The Bang, Bang, Bang

The Bang, Bang, Bang

Roy Glenn

www.urbanbooks.net

Urban Books, LLC
300 Farmingdale Road, N.Y.-Route 109
Farmingdale, NY 11735

The Bang, Bang, Bang Copyright © 2025 Roy Glenn

All rights reserved. No part of this book may be reproduced in any form or by any means without prior consent of the Publisher, except brief quotes used in reviews.

To the extent that the image or images on the cover of this book depict a person or persons, such person or persons are merely models, and are not intended to portray any character or characters featured in the book.

ISBN 13: 978-1-64556-730-1
EBOOK ISBN 978-1-64556-734-9

First Trade Paperback Printing September 2025
Printed in the United States of America

10 9 8 7 6 5 4 3 2 1

This is a work of fiction. Any references or similarities to actual events, real people, living or dead, or to real locales are intended to give the novel a sense of reality. Any similarity in other names, characters, places, and incidents is entirely coincidental.

Distributed by Kensington Publishing Corp.
Submit Orders to:
Customer Service
400 Hahn Road
Westminster, MD 21157-4627
Phone: 1-800-733-3000
Fax: 1-800-659-2436

The authorized representative in the EU for product safety and compliance
Is eucomply OU, Parnu mnt 139b-14, Apt 123
Tallinn, Berlin 11317, hello@eucompliancepartner.com

The Bang, Bang, Bang

Roy Glenn

Chapter 1

"Tell me something that I actually wanna hear. Who hit us?" Terrell Sanders demanded to know. He had just survived an assassination attempt and was in hiding.

"Barbara Ray," Ripley advised.

"Barbara?" Sanders nodded because he had heard the name before.

He had met Barbara one night at the gambling house on Sexton Place when she went there with Mason Grant. He remembered that she was the one who tried to cover the rest of the money that Bellamy owed him when Grant assumed the debt.

"The way I get it, she was the one who sent the people who hit us."

"What else do you know about her?"

"She owns The Playhouse and a boutique."

"A boutique?" Sanders chuckled.

"Yeah, nigga, a boutique. But the guys she sent operate out of The Playhouse."

Sanders nodded, and then he thought about what to do, but there really wasn't much of a choice.

He had to kill Barbara.

"Curtis and Tone with you?"

"Yeah."

"You know where to find her?" Sanders asked.

"She ain't gonna be hard to find."

"Kill her."

"On it," Ripley promised.

After receiving their target and instructions from Ripley, Curtis Fulton and Anthony "Tone" Quinn left the apartment where Sanders was hiding and went after their prey for the night. They were two violent men who made their money robbing drug dealers. Both of them had long arrest records. Fulton had been arrested for attempted murder, sexual assault, kidnapping, assault, carjacking, and motor vehicle theft, while Quinn's record included burglary, simple assault, and battery. He was arrested and charged with involuntary manslaughter when he accidentally fired a gun and killed someone, but the case was dismissed for lack of evidence.

"Who is this bitch?" Tone asked as Curtis drove.

"Does it matter?"

"Not really. I just wanted to know," Tone said as he checked his weapon of choice: a sawed-off, double-barrel pump shotgun. "Let's go do this," he said before getting out of Curtis's Honda Civic.

Curtis walked toward the building where Barbara's office was located, pulling down his mask and taking the two Glock 9 mm handguns he liked carrying. High-End Fashions was closed, and only a few people were in Fat Larry's, the restaurant in the same building Barbara owned. Jolina had gone home for the night, and only Barbara and Tahanee were in the office when Curtis and Tone arrived. They entered the building and went up to the second floor, where the offices were located.

When they entered the office, Tahanee was the first person they saw. She was caught off guard when she looked up and saw the two masked gunmen.

"Oh, shit!" Tahanee shouted when she saw them coming. She was reaching for her gun when Tone raised the pump and fired.

The blast hit Tahanee in the chest, and the impact took her off her feet and blew her into the next room. Her twisted body lay on the floor.

Barbara heard the blast.

"What the fuck?" she said and got up to see what it was, but she got her gun from her desk drawer first.

When she came out of her office, Barbara saw Curtis and Tone coming at her and fired when she saw Tahanee's twisted body on the floor in Destiny's office. Curtis raised both of his weapons and began firing at Barbara. She got off several shots as she ran into the conference room. Curtis and Tone ran behind her, firing.

Barbara dove under the conference room table, turned it over, and came up firing, but the two gunmen had her seriously outgunned. When she stood to return their fire, one of Curtis's bullets hit her in the chest, and Barbara went down. Tone and Curtis took off their masks and stood over Barbara's lifeless body.

"Let's go."

"I know you got someplace to be," Curtis said, laughing as they walked away.

"And I'm already late."

Barbara opened her eyes long enough to get a good look at the two men and promised to kill them before she lost consciousness.

The assassins left the office, and Curtis drove as fast as he could until he got to Purple Rock, the nightclub owned and operated by Rain Robinson. When they arrived, Tone jumped out of the car and ran to the back door. He banged on the door a few times before it opened.

"You're late," the doorman said as Tone entered the building.

"I know," Tone said, rushing past the guard and quickly making his way backstage. He could hear Hayven Kawai on stage and knew from what she was singing that he had missed his mark, and she would be mad at him.

"You're late," the stage manager said.

"I know," Tone replied.

The stage manager signaled to Hayven, and she acknowledged Tone's presence offstage. She gave him an angry look and kept singing. When she nodded, the stage manager told Tone to take his position on stage. When Hayven finished her song, the lights went out.

"Ladies and Gentlemen, Undisputed Truth."

The spotlight appeared on Tone, and he broke into his song to thunderous applause.

Chapter 2

After a long day at the office, Jolina was heading home when she realized she had left her cell phone on her desk and drove back to the office to get it. She brought her Audi R8 to a screeching halt in front of the office, parked the car, and got out. As she walked toward the building, Jolina saw Curtis's Honda Civic speeding away, but she didn't think anything of it at the time. She went into the building, up the stairs, and into the office.

"I know y'all gonna say, how can you forget your phone when you be on it all the time," Jolina said as she entered the office. "Oh my God!" she exclaimed when she saw Tahanee's dead body on the floor. "Tahanee!"

Jolina rushed to the body, saw the damage Tone did with the pump, and began to cry.

"Barbie!" she shouted, rushing to her desk to grab her phone and dial 911. "Barbie!" she shouted again and cried as she frantically searched the office for Barbara. Finally, Jolina saw the table turned over in the conference room. "Barbie!"

When she came around the table, Jolina saw Barbara had been shot as well.

"Oh my God, Barbie!" she shouted and dropped to her knees.

"911 operator. What is your emergency?"

"Two women were shot, and I need an ambulance immediately," Jolina said as the tears flowed freely down her cheeks.

First responders were dispatched once Jolina had given the operator all the information she needed. Jolina ended the call and tried to compose herself as she called RJ. At the time, he was out with Judah. They were making the rounds to check the spots RJ ran for their captain, Sherman Williams.

They were coming out of Mama's Country Kitchen when his phone rang. Although Mama's no longer hosted a gambling operation, a man gotta eat, and the food there was incredible.

RJ took out his phone and glanced at the display. "Jolina," he said in surprise because she had never called him.

"What little sexy want?" Judah asked as they walked to RJ's car.

"I don't know." He swiped talk. "What's up, Jolina?"

"Somebody shot Barbie and Tahanee," she cried, and her tears poured down her cheeks.

"What?" RJ asked in disbelief.

"Somebody shot Barbie and Tahanee," she repeated.

"Are they alive?" RJ asked as he made it to his car.

"I don't know."

He and Judah got in the vehicle. "Where are you?"

"At the office."

"Do you know who did it?"

"No. When I came back to the office to get my phone, that's how I found them."

"Okay. I'm on my way to you." RJ drove fast. "Did you call the police?"

"Ambulance is on the way."

"What happened, Jolina?"

"I had gone for the night, but I had to come back, and that's how I found them," Jolina said, crying. Her entire body ached.

"I'm on my way," RJ said, dropping the phone and driving faster.

"What's wrong?" Judah asked.
"Somebody shot Barbara and Tahanee."
"Are they alive?"
"Jolina didn't know."

When the police got to the building, they took her pulse and pronounced Tahanee dead just as the ambulance arrived and the paramedics entered the scene.

"This one's gone, but there's another body," the officer said, standing up.

"Where?" one of the paramedics asked.

"This way," Jolina said, leading them to the conference room. When they saw the body, they went to work checking Barbara.

"I got a pulse," the paramedic shouted, and they began working on Barbara and got her ready to be transported to the hospital.

"Can you tell me what happened here?" the police officer asked Jolina as the paramedics put Barbara on the wheeled cot.

"No. I came back for my phone, and that's how I found them," Jolina said and began following the paramedics.

"I'm sure the detectives will have more questions for you when they arrive."

Jolina's eyes got wide. "I'm going with her!"

"But—" the cop said to the back of Jolina's head as the paramedics took Barbara down the stairs. She followed the paramedics and watched in tears as they put Barbara into the ambulance.

A cold chill washed over RJ when he turned on the street and saw all the police and emergency vehicles outside the building. Once he parked and exited the car, he and Judah approached the chaotic scene. Then he saw Jolina standing by the ambulance and ran to her. She saw him coming, and her tears began to flow again.

"What happened?"

"Tahanee is dead. They're taking Barbie to the hospital."

"I'm right behind you," RJ said as Jolina climbed into the ambulance. "Where are you taking her?" he shouted.

"Saint Barnabas Hospital," the paramedic replied, shutting the ambulance door.

RJ watched the ambulance drive away and took out his phone as an unmarked car arrived at the crime scene, and Detectives Hudson and Luna got out. RJ recognized them right away.

The relationship between Hudson and Jolina was hot and heavy until then-Lieutenant Dawkins pulled him aside when she got wind of it.

"I can't tell you what to do with your personal life. So, I'll just offer you this tidbit of advice and let it go. Even though she's not a major player in the Family, she is an associate, and that makes her as much of a criminal as the rest of the Family. It doesn't look good for you, an NYPD detective, to conduct an investigation in which the Family is involved if nothing else is on the periphery." Dawkins paused. "Kinda makes you the snitch in our house. I'm not saying you are, but perception is everything."

"I hear you, Lieutenant," Hudson said, and although it hurt him, Jolina was like no other woman he'd ever been involved with, and he thought that he could love and commit to her and only her, he broke it off with her and hadn't seen or spoken to her since.

Hudson had been there once before while involved with Jolina, so he knew that was where Barbara ran her legitimate business. Hudson recognized RJ from the one time he had met him, and RJ nodded to him as he and Luna entered the building. RJ walked away from the building, taking out his phone and approaching his car.

"What's up?" Judah asked.

They got in the car. "Tahanee is dead. They're taking Barbie to the hospital."

"She gonna be all right?"

"I don't know," RJ said.

"She know who did it?"

"No, she doesn't. She said she found them that way."

"My money is on the BBKs," Judah said.

"Yeah. Me too," RJ said and called his parents.

When the phone rang, Bobby and Pam were in his basement mancave watching television. Since his phone rarely rang at this hour of the night these days, Pam's first thought was that it was a woman calling her husband, and her eyes narrowed. Bobby saw the look on her face, smiled because he thought it was funny, and glanced at the display.

"It's your son."

Her facial expression softened into a smile. "I didn't say a word."

"Yeah, but you were thinking it." He swiped talk. "What's up, RJ?" Bobby answered.

"Barbara's been shot."

"Oh, no. Is she all right?"

"She's alive. They're taking her to the hospital. But Tahanee is dead."

"Who did it?" Bobby asked as the anger welled up inside him.

"I don't know, Pop."

"Okay. What hospital are they taking her to?"

Pam could tell by the look in his eyes and the tone of his voice that something was terribly wrong, and when she heard the word "hospital," she feared the worst.

"They're taking her to Saint Barnabas Hospital. Jolina is with her, and I'm following the ambulance."

"Do you know what happened?"

"No, sir, I don't."

"Call Rain. I'm on my way," Bobby said, and he ended the call and looked at Pam.

"What's wrong, Bobby?" Pam asked and braced herself for what she was about to hear.

"Barbara's been shot."

"Oh God," Pam said as her knees gave way, and she tearfully collapsed into Bobby's arms.

"She's alive." He held her tightly as she cried. "They're taking her to Saint Barnabas Hospital. Jolina is with her, and RJ is following the ambulance."

Pam wiped away her tears and stood up. "I'll get Venus and the baby."

"I'll bring the car around."

Suddenly, his legs got weak, and his head began to spin. Bobby took out his phone to call Black.

Chapter 3

Freeport, Grand Bahama Island

After spending a week on vacation in North Island in Seychelles, an island in the Indian Ocean east of Kenia, the Black family headed home. However, instead of flying back to New York, they stopped in Freeport. Napoleon called and said that there was a matter that he needed to discuss with Black. It was late in the evening when Napoleon arrived at the house, and the two men went outside and sat by the pool to talk.

"Several drug gangs have recently come to the island and are creating problems for some of the operators."

"What's Jada's doing about the situation?"

"She's sitting back." Napoleon paused when he saw the look on Black's face. "It's her management style to sit back, take her time, observe, evaluate, and seek counsel before taking decisive action to settle the matter. As one of the people that Ms. West seeks counsel from—"

"As am I."

"I would say that she is still in the evaluation stage."

"And the problem is?"

"Some of those same operators would like Ms. West to jump ahead to the decisive action stage." Napoleon chuckled. "Which they all, to a man, like because Ms. West can be quite brutal when she takes decisive action."

"I am well aware." Black chuckled and sipped his drink. "What's your part in this?"

"Some of the operators sought my counsel, and I promised to bring it to your attention."

"I see." Black nodded. "Have you spoken to Ms. West about the matter?"

"No, I have not." Napoleon got up to pour himself another drink. "My understanding is that she is in New York with Carmen Taylor," he said as Black's phone rang.

"Excuse me. I gotta take this," Black said and accepted the call. "What's up, Granddad?"

"Somebody shot my baby girl, Mike."

"Barbara?"

"Yeah."

"Is she okay?"

"I don't know. They're taking her to the hospital."

"I'm coming, Bob." Black paused as a rush of emotion washed over him. For years, Barbara was like a daughter to him. He couldn't imagine what Bobby was feeling. "You, okay?"

"No, Mike. I am not okay."

"Hold on, Bob. I'm coming. I'm coming as fast as I can." Black ended the call and dialed another number.

"What's wrong?" Napoleon asked.

"Somebody shot Barbara."

"Is she all right?" he asked as Jake answered the phone.

"What's up, Boss?"

"Get the jet ready. We're leaving."

"You got it," Jake said, and Black ended the call.

"Is she all right?" Napoleon asked again.

"Bobby doesn't know. He said they're taking her to the hospital."

They went back into the house, and Black saw Napoleon out. Then he went to tell Shy. She could tell by how he was walking and the look on his face that something was wrong.

"What's wrong, Michael?" she asked.

"Somebody shot Barbara."

"Is she all right?"

"I don't know. Bobby said they were taking her to the hospital. We need to get the family ready to travel."

Once they had repacked what little they had unpacked, Black and Shy brought their luggage to the door. Michelle was the first to arrive at the door with her luggage. Black took it out to the car.

"Something on your mind?" Shy asked.

"Just thinking about Barbara. You know, hoping she's OK."

"Me too."

Michelle looked at her mother and took a deep breath. "I was thinking about something Barbara said."

Shy sat down on the stairs. "What's that?"

Michelle sat beside her mother. "She said that you're a wife, a mother, a businesswoman, and you're cool Aunt Shy. But let something happen, and your mother turns into your father."

Shy smiled. "She did?"

"She did. And I'm having a problem reconciling."

Shy smiled. She loved that she and Michelle were getting on better terms. "Why is that?"

"Because it's not the image I have of you." Michelle paused. "From what I've seen growing up in this family is that you get yourself into trouble, and Daddy gets you out of it."

Shy laughed. "Many times that is the case. But your father knows when to step back and let me handle my business my way."

"I've just never seen that."

"Let me put it to you this way. You know who and what your father was and still is when he chooses to be." Michelle nodded, and Shy continued. "There are people who say you can fill a cemetery with all the people your father has personally killed. But has he ever talked to you about a single one?"

Michelle paused to think. Much of what she knew, she knew because she used to listen at doors. "No, he never has."

"So, using that same logic—" Shy encouraged Michelle to find her own way.

"Why should I expect you to," Michelle said, nodding her understanding. "It's just not the picture I have of you."

"Michelle, I'm your mother, and I love you. I know how you feel about your father and your respect and admiration for him. But I wanted you to respect and admire me because I was a good mother to you and your brothers." Shy giggled. "Not because of how dope I am with a Beretta."

"You have a gun?" a wide-eyed Michelle asked.

Shy stood up. "Go get your brother ready to travel. I'm going to check on the 'Golden Girls.'"

Michelle stood up. "You didn't answer my question."

"I'll show you when we return to the city." Shy left the room but stuck her head in. "Maybe you'll show me yours."

"Huh?"

"I said, maybe you'll show me yours. You know. The one your father gave you on your fifteenth birthday," Shy said, walking away.

The Bronx, New York

After making the hour's drive into the city from Rockland County, Bobby and Pam arrived at the hospital, along with Venus and the baby. They were promptly informed that Barbara was in surgery and told that they could wait in the waiting room. RJ bounced up when he saw them coming. He hugged each of his parents, kissed Venus, and took his son from her arms.

"What happened?" Bobby demanded to know.

"Jolina called me and told me about it," RJ said, pointing to Jolina, sitting alone with her head in her hands. She was taking it badly. Her eyes were red from all the tears she'd cried.

"You know who did it?" Bobby asked.

"I don't know, but the BBKs would be my guess."

It was then that Destiny and Kayla arrived in the waiting room and rushed to Jolina. Bobby watched the tear-filled group hug.

"I need to talk to her," Bobby said and approached them. "Jolina?"

"Yes, Mr. Ray." Jolina tried as best she could to wipe away her tears.

"Can you tell me what happened?"

"We were working late, and I had gone home, but I had to return because I forgot my phone. When I arrived, that's how I found them."

"Do you have any idea who might have done this? Anybody Barbara was having problems with that you know of?"

"No, sir. All we've been doing is building Barbie's legitimate businesses."

"Anything out of the ordinary in that?"

"No, sir," Jolina said, and then she paused. "The only thing I can think of is that she and Tahanee met with Jada West and Carmen Taylor. There was some kind of issue."

"Issue? What kind of issue?"

"It was enough of an issue that Barbie called Jackie, and she ordered us to treat Ms. West with all the respect that her position in this Family affords her."

"Jada and Carmen, huh?" Bobby thought about the combination and their penchant for getting themselves in trouble. "What came of that?"

"I don't know. I wasn't in the meeting," Jolina said as the nurse approached RJ in the waiting room.

"Thank you, Jolina," Bobby said, walking away to hear what the nurse had to say. Jolina followed them.

"Mr. Ray?" The nurse asked RJ.

"Yes. These are my parents, Mr. and Mrs. Ray."

"How's my baby?" Pam asked.

"Your daughter is going to be fine. The doctor had a second surgery to perform, but he promised to talk to you as soon as possible. She was fortunate. The bullet went through and didn't hit any major organs or arteries."

"Oh, thank God," Pam said, and Bobby held her tighter.

"Can we see her?" Bobby asked.

"She's in recovery now, but as soon as she's assigned a room, I will come and get you."

"Thank you," Bobby said, and they sat down as the nurse left the waiting area.

Shortly after that, Detectives Hudson and Luna arrived in the waiting room to talk to Jolina. He looked around the waiting room until their eyes met. It was apparent that despite the circumstances, each was glad to see the other.

"You ready for this?" Luna asked, seeing the way that they were looking at each other.

"Sure, why wouldn't I be?"

"You really need me to answer that?"

"No, you don't have to answer. But I'm good."

"You sure? Because I could talk to her if you want."

"No, I'm okay." The detective took a deep breath.

"OK, let's go do this," Luna said and started for Jolina.

"Let me talk to her alone," he said as they approached Jolina.

"You sure that's a good idea?"

"No. But she might be more open with me," Hudson said, walking away from his partner.

"Hello, Jolina."

"How are you, Darius?"

"I'm sorry about Barbara. Do you know how she's doing?"

"The nurse said that the bullet went through and didn't hit any major organs, so she's going to be fine."

"I'm glad to hear that." He paused. "I need to ask you some questions, but we can do that another time if you're not feeling up to it."

"No, I'm all right."

"Do you mind if I sit?"

Jolina extended her hand graciously to the seat next to her.

"Thank you," Hudson said and sat down.

A chill washed over him, being that close to her. He tried to shake it off, but the feeling was inescapable.

"Can you walk me through what happened tonight?"

Jolina exhaled because she was tired of telling the story. "Me, Barbie, and Tahanee had worked late, as usual, and I had gone home, but I left my cell phone and returned for it. When I got back, that's how I found them."

"And you did see anybody?"

"No, I didn't."

"Can you tell me what Barbara was into? I know the Family was going at it with the BBKs. Do you think they were involved in some way?"

"I can't say for sure, but I don't think so. Barbie's been working on building her legitimate businesses and didn't have any part in the war. Honestly, I think she was happier going legit."

"Anything else you can tell me?"

Jolina paused. "There is something."

"What's that?"

"When I arrived, I saw a grey Honda drive away fast. I didn't think anything of it at the time, but now . . . It might be the people who did it."

"Did you see who was driving?"

"No."

"You know what year Honda it was?"

Jolina shook her head. "Sorry, I'm not a car person."

"Thank you, Jolina." Hudson was about to get up.

"You know you broke my heart, but I understood," Jolina giggled. "To tell you the truth, I got the same talk from Barbara."

Hudson smiled and looked into Jolina's soft eyes. "To tell *you* the truth, it was the hardest thing I ever had to do. I was so into you."

"But they were right. It didn't look good for either of us."

"Especially with the task force investigating the Family."

Joline leaned a little closer. "Maybe now that you're not on the task force and not investigating the Family and Barbie has gone legit, we can see each other."

Hudson looked around for Luna. She was talking to Bobby and Pam.

"I'd like that." He stood up. "Thank you for speaking to me, Jolina," he said in a very professional manner. "If I have any questions, I'll contact you."

"I'd like that too," she said softly.

Chapter 4

The Black family arrived at Westchester County Airport and headed straight to Saint Barnabas Hospital. When he arrived in the waiting room, Bobby told him Barbara would be all right.

"Oh, thank God," Shy said and hugged Pam.

At that point, Black only had one question.

"Now, tell me who did it?" he asked, looking around the room at the assembled Family members.

After a brief silence, Bobby said, "We don't know yet."

"What do you know?"

Bobby shook his head. "Not much." He paused and then pointed. "Jolina found the bodies. Tahanee was dead when she got there."

"What was Barbara into?"

"Nobody knows that either," Bobby said.

"Barbara was focused on building her legitimate business," Michelle volunteered.

"The consensus opinion is that it was the BBKs, Uncle Mike," RJ said.

"The only other thing was that she met with Jada West and Carmen Taylor," Bobby added.

"Jada and Carmen? Why would Barbara have a meeting with them?"

"Jolina didn't know. She wasn't in the meeting," Bobby replied.

"Anybody know why Jada is in the city?" Black asked and looked around for Rain, who was conspicuously absent.

"I didn't even know she was in the city," Bobby said.

Black took out his phone and made a call.

"This is Jackie."

"Where are you?"

"At Conversations."

"Stay there. I'm coming to you."

"Good. I have something that I need to tell you."

"At least somebody does."

"You at the hospital?"

"Yes."

"How's Barbara?"

"She's going to be fine. Bullet went through."

"That's good to hear. See you when you get here," Jackie said, and Black ended the call.

"Let's go, Bob."

"I'm good here for the time being," he said, squeezing Pam's hand.

"I understand." Black stood up and RJ, Marvin, Baby Chris, and Judah stood when he did. "I guess y'all are with me," he said to The Four Kings. "Let's go," and they left the hospital.

Shortly after Black left with The Four Kings, Rain arrived at the hospital. She went and sat down with Bobby and Pam, and he told her what she had missed.

"Where were you anyway?" Bobby asked.

"I had a meeting. I'll tell you about it another time."

"See that you do," Bobby said.

Rain was late getting to the hospital because she was meeting with Sherman Williams and one of his numbers runners, Shayla Clark. She also ran a little loan sharking when her cash and the opportunity presented themselves. Her brother, Marchello Clark, a gambler and enforcer for Judah, overheard a plot by Byron White to kill Sherman and RJ because he felt his father, Clarence White, a.k.a. Whitey, should have been made captain when Doc was assassinated.

It all began years ago on the night Black gave his now famous treason speech and the very public execution of Gary Banks.

"I like the British laws on treason better than the American. So, I consider selling drugs to be a serious threat to the stability or continuity of this organization."

All of a sudden, Bobby grabbed Banks and held his arms. Black hit him in the face. Once, twice, three, four times.

"Gary Banks," Black said and hit him again, "you're being charged—" Black hit him again, "with treason." He hit Banks a final time. Bobby let Banks go, and he fell to the floor.

The brutal execution sent shock waves throughout the Family, with the implications lasting to this very day and shaping the Family for years to come.

That night, Black put Doc in charge of that spot, which came to be known as Doc's as the years passed. However, that wasn't the only thing that happened that night. When it was over, Whitey, came and sat down next to Doc. Needless to say, Doc was understandably still shaken by the ordeal he had just witnessed and was almost a part of.

"Bet you were thinking you were gonna die along with Banks," Whitey said.

"Yeah, I did." Doc stood up. "I need a drink."

"Make it two," Whitey said and followed Doc to the bar.

That night, a friendly rivalry began between the two. Therefore, when Black made Doc a captain, naturally, Whitey thought that he should have gotten the nod. So, when Doc was murdered, naturally, Whitey thought that Black should have made him captain . . . but that didn't happen either.

It was decided to split Doc's crew between Carter Garrison and Sherman Williams, who had recently come out of retirement at Black's request. Since they were a better fit, most of Doc's business went to Sherman, something that didn't sit well with Whitey. That animosity poured over to his son, Byron, who had a plan to seize power now that his father was advancing in age and poor health.

"Marchello overheard Byron and Giovanni Folliero talking about the plot to kill RJ and Sherman, so they killed him. Long story short, Shayla killed Byron and Giovanni Folliero. The problem is that Folliero is a made guy with the Montanari family."

Rain dropped her head. "Damn."

"Yeah," Sherman said. "Now, they want *her* head."

"What about Whitey?"

"I took care of that myself," Sherman said, and Rain nodded her approval.

"I'll take care of it. In the meantime, you need to lie low, Shayla. Understood?"

"Yes, Rain. And I'm sorry for bringing this kind of heat on the Family."

"I get it. They killed your brother. You did know that he was a made guy. But that's what you got a captain for. You should have talked to Sherman before you went after them. But what's done is done." Rain stood up. "I'm going to the hospital." She looked at Sherman. "You coming, old man?"

"I'm gonna sit this one out. If Mike's back in the city, tell him I need to speak to him," Sherman said.

"I'll let him know."

Shy sat in the hospital waiting room with Rain, Bobby, and Pam, while Michelle sat with Jolina, Destiny, and Kayla. They were talking about how secretive Barbara and Tahanee had been lately, so she had no idea what was happening, and then Jolina mentioned that Barbara and Tahanee had met with Carmen Taylor and Jada West, and, for obvious reasons, it piqued Shy's curiosity.

"Excuse me, Pam," Shy said and stood up. Jolina, Destiny, and Kayla stopped talking when they saw Shy coming.

"Excuse me, ladies."

"Yes, Mrs. Black."

"Did you say that Barbara and Tahanee had a meeting with Carmen Taylor and Jada West?"

"Yes, ma'am."

"You know what it was about?"

"No, I'm sorry, Mrs. Black, but I don't. They were secretive, so I had no idea what was happening."

"Thank you," Shy said, returning to where Rain sat with Bobby and Pam. "Let me holla at you for a second, Rain."

Rain got up and followed Shy away from the Rays. "What's up?" she asked, and Shy told her about the meeting with Jada and Carmen.

"Why would Barbara and Tahanee meet with Carmen Taylor and Jada West?" Rain asked.

"I don't know, but I'd sure like to find out." Shy smiled at Rain. "What are you getting ready to do?"

"Nothing, why?" Rain giggled. "You want me to ride with you so you don't kill them?"

"Something like that."

"Let's go."

"Michelle."

"Yes, Mommy."

"See to it that your grandmothers and your brothers get home safely."

"Yes, Mommy. Where are you going?" Michelle asked.

"Going to handle my business my way," Shy said. "Let's go, Rain."

Chapter 5

When Black arrived with The Four Kings, as it always was, Conversations was packed and jumping. They were escorted to the office, where Jackie, Axe, and Press were waiting. After handshakes and high fives, Black sat down on the couch.

"Who shot Barbara?" Black asked.

"Axe," Jackie said, and all eyes turned to him.

"Barbara and Tahanee had me and Press following Carmen Taylor."

"Why?"

"Carmen Taylor was investigating Mason Grant's murder, and Barbara wanted to know what she found out. So, our *orders* were to follow her and question everybody she talked to."

"Why would Barbara want to know about who killed Mason Grant?" Black asked.

"Does he need to spell it out for you, Black?" Jackie asked.

Black thought for a second or two. "Oh," he said and chuckled when it finally hit him. He smiled uncomfortably and nodded. "Go on, Axe."

At that point, Axe thought it best to cover his and Press's asses.

"When I saw that Carmen Taylor was riding with Jada West, I called Tahanee and told her, you know, 'cause Jada West is a captain, and I didn't think that was something we needed to be doing," Axe said, and Press nodded.

"But Tahanee said it was cool, so we kept following them. That lasted until Ms. West spotted us and came at us with a gun in her hand."

"Ms. West is sharp and is not to be fucked with." Black laughed. "What did she say?"

Axe cleared his throat. "She said, 'Perhaps you care to tell me why you and Mr. Preston are following Ms. Taylor and me.' I said we're just following orders, Ms. West. And she wanted to know whose orders those would be, and when I told her that we were following Barbara's orders, she told me that I was going to call her *now* and find out where Barbara was and tell her to expect a visit from her. 'Do you understand, Mr. Brinson?'" Axe recounted.

"And what did you say?" Black asked. By that time, both he and Jackie were laughing.

"Yes, ma'am, I understand."

"Okay," Black chuckled. "Now I know why they met. What was the meeting about?"

"I don't know, Mr. Black."

"So, I'm gonna ask this question one more time. And this time, I want an answer. Who shot Barbara?"

"We think that Terrell Sanders is behind it," Axe said.

"Why?" Black asked.

"Because after it came out that his manager, Willard Bellamy, was responsible, Barbara sent us to kill Terrell Sanders."

"What did Sanders have to do with Grant and Bellamy?"

"Carmen told her that Jessica Tate, the Chosen Few Production Studio CFO, had stolen close to a million dollars, and it threw the company into complete disarray," Jackie began. "Bellamy had a bank loan that he didn't want to default on, so he went to Sanders for money to cover the loan. When Grant learned about the $500,000 loan, he assumed the debt. The way Barbara saw it, the two people, Willard Bellamy and Terrell Sanders, were responsible for Grant's murder, and she would have her revenge against both of them."

"That was when Barbara sent us to kill Terrell Sanders, but he got away." Axe paused. "I think she hired a shooter to kill Willard Bellamy," Axe added.

"She did," Jackie confirmed. "She arranged it with Fiona."

Black shook his head. "She is definitely her father's daughter." He looked at RJ. "You know about this?"

"I knew about her and Grant, but the rest of this is news to me, Uncle Mike."

"I want this nigga found, and I want him and anybody that's down with him dead," Black said and looked around the office at The Four Kings. "Fuck y'all standing around for? Bring me this nigga's head."

"Yes, sir," The Four Kings, Axe, and Press all said and departed.

When they did, Black dropped his head into the palms of his hands.

Jackie giggled. "You okay?"

"No." Black looked up. "It's gonna take me a minute or two to wrap my head around this."

"See what you miss when you go on vacation? How was it, anyway?" Jackie asked.

"Great. Me and Cassandra got to spend some time together, the boys had a ball, and Michelle was bored out of her mind."

"No one her age to hang out with?"

"Oh, no, there were plenty of people her age, but she said the white girls were too snobby, and she wasn't into the white boys who were following her around every place. She said they were too anxious and too stupid."

Jackie laughed. "I'm sure you didn't mind that."

"Not at all. Better her bored than the alternative. I need a drink," Black said and stood up. "You know, for years before Michelle was born, I looked at Barbara as my daughter too," he said as he poured.

"I didn't know that."

"I did. So, the idea of Barbara being sexual . . ." He shook his head, "is foreign to me." He chuckled. "I don't even wanna think about Michelle like that. So, to find out that our little girl was fucking Mason Grant, and the dick was so good to her that she took the steps she did, following Carmen and Jada and ordering hits . . . Yeah, Jackie, it's gonna take me a minute." Black shot his drink. "I'm glad Bobby decided to stay at the hospital," Black said, but he knew he would have to tell Bobby about his baby girl.

Chapter 6

As they walked away from the hospital to Rain's car, Shy took out her phone and made the call.

"Jada, it's Shy," she began. "Are you still in the city?"

"Not for long. Carmen and I will be leaving for Barcelona soon. What's up?"

"I need to talk to you."

"I'm at The Mansion waiting for you."

"See you in a while," Shy said, getting in the car with Rain. "She's at The Mansion."

"On our way," Rain said and started the car. "You and Jada seem to get along." She laughed. "I remember the days when your knife would come out at the mere mention of her name."

"I wouldn't call it 'getting along.'"

"What would you call it?"

"Coexistence." Shy paused. "It took me a minute to really accept and believe that Michael isn't interested in her. Like he said, if he wanted her, he would have her, and his interest in her is strictly business."

"Bitch does know how to make money," Rain commented.

"For a long time, I was just giving lip service to believing that he never loved her. That they were just business partners and the sex just happened." Shy pointed to herself. "That was my own lack of confidence in myself after being away for so long." She giggled. "At least that's what my shrink says."

"I didn't know you were seeing somebody."

"I spent three years on an island talking to myself. I was a little fucked up in the head. I still have nightmares about my experience."

"I never knew."

"It wasn't like I was about to broadcast it to the Family."

"I hear you. And you know this stays between us."

"Thanks, Rain, but I would expect no less."

"Shit, sometimes, I think I need to see somebody, talk through my shit."

"Give it a try. You have nothing to lose." There was silence in the car as Rain considered it. "So, what's up with you and Carter?"

"Nothing. We barely speak to each other. We used to have so much to say to each other, and I know it's my fault."

"How so?"

"I don't wanna hear shit he has to say." Rain laughed. "I've had four serious relationships in my life. And every one of them dogged and cheated on me relentlessly and lied to my face about it. With Ronnie King, I was young, stupid, and didn't know any better. Shit, Nick proved to me that I may have gotten older, but I was just as stupid. He was fucking Danielle, Mercedes, and Tasheka right damn near in front of my face. And Dr. Von Preston—come to find out that nigga was fucking any and everyone with a pulse."

"I'm sorry."

"Yeah, me too. So, when I hooked up with Carter, it was gonna be just sex because, girl, let me tell you, that nigga packs a punch. But Carter Garrison is like any man with a big, fat, juicy dick."

"How is that?" Shy wanted to know since she was married to a man with a big, fat, juicy dick.

"They know they have a big dick, and they want to share it with as many women as possible. So, I should have known better, but I caught feelings for him, and then I got pregnant." Rain paused and thought for a second or two before she angrily said, "So, here I am, pregnant with the nigga's baby, and I fuck around and find out this muthafucka fuckin' Fantasy."

"I'm sorry," was all that Shy could say.

"Yeah, me too. So now, I'm taking a serious break from men." Rain glanced over at Shy. "And no, I ain't started suckin' pussy. I go to the gym, focus on my training in Beom Seogi Taekwondo, and have meaningless sex with men I don't know."

"Yeah, girl, maybe talking to somebody would do you some good," Shy said as they arrived at The Mansion. It was a house of gambling and prostitution that Jada opened in New York to rival Paraiso in Nassau. Rain allowed her car to be valet-parked, and they approached the house.

Since The Mansion was Jada's establishment, her men had no idea who Rain and Shy were, and they were not members of the exclusive club.

"State your business," the doorman said.

"Cassandra Black and Rain Robinson to see Jada West," Shy said, and his eyes got big. He quickly signaled for another staff member.

"Good evening, Mrs. Black, Ms. Robinson, and welcome to The Mansion," he said formally as a woman dressed in white joined him. He whispered in her ear, and her eyes opened wide.

"Good evening, Mrs. Black and Ms. Robinson, and welcome to The Mansion," she said formally. "If you would like to follow me, I will escort you to Ms. West."

When they arrived at Jada's office, their escort knocked and opened the door.

"Excuse me, Ms. West." Jada stood up wearing a fuchsia-black Amsale gown. "I have Cassandra Black and Rain Robinson to see you."

"By all means, show them in," Jada said, and she opened the door for them to enter the office. "Good evening, ladies. I have to say, this is unexpected, which leads me to ask, is there a problem?"

"Barbara's been shot."

"Oh my goodness," Jada exclaimed. "Is she going to be all right?"

"Yes," Shy said. "The bullet went through her."

"Thank God."

"We were hoping to talk to Carmen about her investigation into Mason Grant's murder and how it relates to Barbara."

"I see. Unfortunately, Carmen is in Atlanta. I expect her back tomorrow because, as I said, she and I are going to Barcelona. However, I was with her every step of the way, so I would be more than happy to share what I know."

"Thank you, Jada," Shy began. "Why did you and Carmen meet with Barbara?"

"Barbara was having an affair with Mason Grant," she said . . . and mouths dropped open wide. "And she had two of her men following us to see who we talked to, and then they would question them and report to Barbara."

"What did Carmen tell Barbara?" Rain asked.

"Without getting into the more salacious details, Mr. Grant believed that his partner, Willard Bellamy, was severely mismanaging the company's finances, and they were on the verge of bankruptcy. However, it resulted from the company CFO, Jessica Tate, stealing a million dollars. Bellamy had a bank loan that he didn't want to default on, so he went to Mr. Sanders for money to cover the loan."

"Do you know where we can find Terrell Sanders?" Shy asked.

Jada picked up the phone on her desk. "Victor, please come to my office. Mrs. Black and Ms. Robinson would like to ask you some questions."

"Right away."

"When his name came up, and he was a known gambler, I had Victor make some inquiries."

"Good evening, ladies. What can I do for you?" Victor asked when he entered the office.

"Would you please tell Mrs. Black and Ms. Robinson what you learned about Mr. Sanders?"

"What I can give you is a gambler named Jacob Fiske. He's one of Sanders's associates. You can find him at the club called Norte el Soul. Ask for Alicia Hall, and there's his girlfriend, a drug dealer named Cherlynn Jushawn. Here's her address. If he's lying low, chances are he's with one of those three."

"Wouldn't happen to have a picture of him, would you?" Shy asked.

"He's on Facebook," Victor said.

"I'm not on Facebook," Shy replied.

"I am," Rain said, taking out her phone, and Shy looked surprised that Rain was on the site. She logged in and went to Jacob Fiske's profile page. "That him?" she asked Victor.

Victor leaned close to look. "That's him. Scroll down," he requested, and Rain scrolled down the page. "And that's Cherlynn Jushawn."

"What about Sanders?" Shy asked.

"Go to her page. Her and Sanders are her profile picture."

"Got it. We out," Rain said.

"Thank you, Victor," Shy said. "And thank you, Jada."

Jada smiled. "My pleasure. Anything I can do for my Family is my honor and privilege."

Chapter 7

Meanwhile, outside Conversations, Black's men were discussing a course of action to accomplish the objective set by Black.

"So, where do we find this nigga?" RJ asked.

"Only place we know is his gambling house on Sexton Place," Axe said.

"But we hit that a couple of days ago. I doubt if they're back up and running," Press added.

"That's all you got?" Judah asked.

"Where did you get that from?" Marvin asked.

"Tahanee told us about the house," Press said.

"If Barbara was fuckin' with Grant, Tahanee would know everything about him and the people he came in contact with," RJ said.

"But Tahanee is dead. So, what now?" Baby Chris asked.

"We roll by the gambling house on Sexton Place and see what's up there," RJ said, and the men separated.

Things looked quiet when Axe, Press, and The Four Kings arrived at the gambling house on Sexton Place, where Terrell Sanders ran his gambling operation. Once they had parked their cars, the men assembled outside the home.

"This is it," Axe stated.

"Doesn't seem much is going on inside. Not as many cars parked out here as the last time we were here," Press added.

"Let's check it out anyway," RJ said.

The six men drew and checked their weapons before following RJ to the house. He knocked on the door, expecting the doorman to answer. When nobody answered, RJ tried the doorknob and found it unlocked. The men entered the house and found that it was back up and running with new people. The last time they were there, poker was being played in one room, blackjack in another, roulette and craps tables were also in separate rooms. That night, only one poker game was going on with five players. The rest of the house was empty.

"I'm looking for Terrell Sanders," RJ said.

"Who?"

RJ moved toward him quickly, grabbed him by the throat, and shoved the barrel of his gun into the man's mouth. Baby Chris pulled both his weapons and pointed them at the other men.

"You don't want none of this."

"You and I both know this is Sanders's spot. Now, tell me where to find him, or I will pull the trigger and blow the back of your head out. What's it gonna be?"

"I don't know where he is. He's been lying low since Barbara Ray sent people to kill him."

RJ cocked the hammer. "You tell Terrel Sanders that I'm going to kill him when I find him," he said and let go of the man, who quickly reached for his throat and gasped for air. Black's men left the house.

"Uncle Mike said to kill everybody down with Sanders," Judah pointed out when they got outside.

"I know what he said," RJ replied.

"So what now?" Marvin asked.

"Axe, you, and Press hang around here, see if Sanders shows up. If not, follow the houseman when he comes out," RJ ordered.

"You got it," Axe said.

"The rest of us will be in the streets," RJ said.

"Too bad the team is in Juba. Carla would have been up on their phone," Marvin said.

"Yeah, 'cause I'm betting as soon as we walk out, that nigga called Sanders," Baby Chris added.

"Yeah, well, the team *is* in Juba, so we gotta find this nigga the old-fashioned way," RJ said.

"One busted head at a time," Press stated.

Chapter 8

Shy and Rain arrived at Norte el Soul, the club where Victor told them they could find people who could lead them to Sanders. Both women checked their weapons before exiting the vehicle and going inside. The place wasn't crowded when they walked in and looked around. Rain immediately identified the exits. Then they walked up to a server.

"I'm looking for Alicia Hall. She here?" Rain asked.

"Alicia—" the server looked around. "There she is." She pointed to a woman in a beach-colored minidress and way too much makeup. "Sitting at that table by herself."

"Thanks," Shy said and gave her a twenty.

"Thank you," the server replied.

Shy and Rain walked over and stood in front of the table. Alicia Hall looked up and rolled her eyes.

"What you bitches want?"

"We're looking for Jacob Fiske. You know where we can find him?" Rain asked.

Alicia smiled. "What's it worth to you?"

Shy glanced at Rain and went into her purse. She put a fifty-dollar bill on the table, and Alicia rolled her eyes. Shy and Rain looked at each other, and Shy put another fifty on the table.

"He's at the bar there," Alicia said, pointing with one hand while grabbing the money with the other. "Brown shirt and jeans."

"Thanks," Shy said, and they went to the bar to talk to Jacob Fiske. As they approached, both women took out their weapons as they drew nearer. They walked up behind him.

"You Jacob Fiske?" Rain asked.

Fiske turned toward them. "Who's asking?"

"Since I'm the one standing in front of you talking, I guess I'm asking."

Fiske seemed amused by her answer and cracked a smile. "What you want?"

"We're looking for Terrell Sanders. You know where to find him?"

"Who?"

Rain chuckled. "I'm in a good mood, so I'm gonna ask you one more time. We're looking for Terrell Sanders. You know where to find him?"

"Fuck—" Before Fiske could say "you," Rain shoved her gun into his mouth.

"Now, I'm not in a good mood. So, I'm gonna ease this gun out of your mouth, and you are gonna tell me where I can find Terrell Sanders."

"Rain," Shy said as two men approached them from either side.

Rain looked at the men approaching and pulled the trigger. Shy shot one, and Rain shot the other. Then Rain looked around the bar at the shocked customers.

"I'm looking for Terrell Sanders. I know somebody here is dying to tell me where he is."

Shy looked around the bar and walked over to where Alicia Hall was sitting. She put a gun to her head.

"What about you? You wanna tell me where to find him?"

"I haven't seen him since somebody sent men to kill him. He's hiding out with Cherlynn Jushawn."

"Thanks," Shy said, and they headed for the exit.

Their next stop was the home of Cherlynn Jushawn. Rain parked, and they were about to get out when somebody came out of the house carrying a suitcase and a shopping bag.

"Hold up, Rain. I think that's her," Shy said.

As Cherylynn loaded the car, Rain took out her phone and opened Facebook.

"That's her."

Once the car was loaded, Cherylynn got in and drove off. Rain and Shy followed her. An hour and a half later, they were in Rock Hill, New York, a hamlet in Sullivan County with a population of fewer than 3,000 people. Soon, they found themselves on Wurtsboro Mountain Road. Rain parked the car down the street from the house where Cherylynn parked and watched as she talked briefly to the man stationed outside the house before she went inside.

Rain got her binoculars. "One man outside. Ain't no telling how many are inside. I'd rather not rush in there blind."

Shy laughed. "You don't wanna rush in?"

"No, Shy, I don't. I would much rather get closer. See what's inside before I rush in and kill everybody."

"*That* sounds more like you," Shy giggled.

"Thank you." Rain looked through her binoculars again. "You still go to the shooting range?"

"Yeah, why?"

"You think you can hit him from here?"

"Not with this Beretta. Maybe with the PLR22."

"I got something for that," Rain said, opening the trunk to reveal her arsenal.

"Damn, Rain," Shy said, looking at the array of weapons.

"I hate being outgunned."

"I see this."

Rain got the Remington 700 XCR long-range rifle with a silencer and handed it to Shy.

"I'm not good with a long gun, but I keep this for Monika."

Shy took the weapon and set it up on the hood of the car. She looked in the scope and acquired her target. As Rain looked through her binoculars, Shy lined up her target and pulled the trigger.

"You missed."

"He moved."

Hearing the sound, the man pulled his gun and looked frantically in all directions. Not seeing anyone, he slowly lowered his weapon and resumed his position. Shy reacquired her target and pulled the trigger once she had the shot lined up. This time, her shot was true and hit him in the chest. He went down.

"Good shot," Rain said, taking the Remington from Shy and putting it back into the trunk. "Let's go."

Rain and Shy approached the house carefully and looked in the window.

"I don't see anybody," Shy said, readying her weapon.

Rain kicked in the door, and they rushed into the empty living room. Rain went left toward the kitchen, while Shy went right. She kicked in the door and ran into the room. Cherlynn was in the bed alone, but the sliding glass door in the bedroom was open.

"He's going out the back!" Shy shouted and shot Cherlynn in the head before running out the back door.

When she got to the front of the house, Shy saw Rain running down the street, exchanging fire with Sanders. She ran to the car, got in, started it up, and went after them. It didn't take her long to catch up with and pass Rain. Shy closed in on Sanders and hit him with the car. His body flew up in the air and hit the ground hard.

Shy stopped the car in front of him as Rain caught up. She got out of the car, and both women approached Sanders's body. Then they raised their weapons and fired.

Chapter 9

Black shot the rest of his drink and stood up. His head was still spinning over the news of the relationship between Barbara and Mason Grant. It made him think about Michelle, and since he never wanted to think along those lines, he quietly pushed thoughts about Michelle being sexually active to the back of his mind and slammed the door shut.

"I'm out," he said.

"Where you on your way to?" Jackie asked, and she got up to escort him out of her office.

"I'm going to talk to Jada and Carmen."

"You think their meeting is related to Barbara getting shot?"

"I don't know. But there are some things I need to discuss with Ms. West," Black said as they exited Jackie's office. When they did, William stood up. "Let's go."

"Good night, Mr. Black."

"Good night, Fiona," Black said, and William blew her a kiss.

"You let me know what Jada says about the meeting," Jackie said and pressed the button for her elevator. The doors opened, and Black and William got on.

"I will," Black said as the doors closed.

Once they reached the ground floor, they made their way through the crowd and left Conversations.

"Where to, Boss?" William asked when they got in the car.

"I'll let you know." Black took out his phone and made a call.

"Good evening, Mr. Black," Jada answered.

"Good evening, Ms. West. Are you still in the city?" Black inquired.

"I'm at The Mansion."

"I have some things I need to talk to you about."

"Come on out. I'll be here waiting for you."

"See you in a while." Black ended the call. "Take me to The Mansion."

"On our way."

Upon arrival at The Mansion, William tossed the keys to the parking lot attendant and followed Black inside. He went directly to Jada's office and knocked on the door.

"Come in. Good evening, Mr. Black."

"Good evening, Ms. West. How are you?"

"I'm great, and you?" Black shook his head and headed toward the bar to pour a drink. "Let me get that for you," she said and went behind the bar. He sat in the chair in front of Jada's desk.

"Tired. It's been a long day."

"I can only imagine," Jada said, pouring him a glass of Rémy Martin Louis XIII.

She handed him his drink.

"Thank you."

"How's Barbara?" Jada asked as she went to sit down.

"I haven't talked to Bobby since I left the hospital, but she's gonna be fine. The bullet went through her."

"That's good. So, what did you want to speak about?"

"I wanted to know why you and Carmen met with Barbara." Black took a sip. "Where is Carmen, anyway?"

"She's back in Atlanta taking care of some business. But she'll be back soon. If nothing else happens, we are vacationing in Barcelona." Jada paused for a moment. "I might as well tell you because you'll hear about it eventually. Carmen is moving back to New York."

"I'm sorry, but I'm not surprised. Carmen isn't built to be Marcus's trophy wife or anchor desk jockey."

"No, she most certainly is not." Jada giggled. "She was in her glory, investigating and solving Mason Grant's murder."

"Is her investigation why you two met with Barbara?"

"Yes, it was. As you probably already know, Barbara was involved in a relationship with Mr. Grant and wanted information about the investigation, which Carmen was glad to share with her."

"About Terrell Sanders?"

"No, she was the one who told Carmen about Sanders. Carmen eventually informed Ms. Ray about Bellamy's involvement in the matter."

Black chuckled. "That information led her to put out a contract on Willard Bellamy and send men to kill Terrell Sanders."

Jada giggled. "Like father, like daughter."

"Did she tell her where to find him?"

"No. However, being a gambler, I had Victor check him out."

"And?"

"He shared that information with your wife and Ms. Robinson."

"Cassandra and Rain were here?"

"They got the information that Victor had and left here more than an hour ago." Jada giggled. "Knowing those two, Mr. Sanders might be dead by now."

"He might be." Black nodded. "There's something else I wanted to talk to you about. On the way back, I stopped in Freeport to talk to Napoleon, who told me about an issue in Nassau. What's going on?"

"The problem is that nothing is going on." Jada stood up, got Black's glass, and returned to the bar. "The last couple of hurricanes did a lot of damage, and foreign investment dollars have not been forthcoming." She poured Black another drink and a French 75 for herself.

"Not surprising. Climate change is real, and chances are another hurricane will hit the islands next year. I suspect some of those investment dollars went into building a resort in Saint Vincent."

"An island not in every hurricane path."

"I'm sure."

"As a consequence, the government cut spending, including cuts to police services, so crime has increased around the hotels. Tourism is down. I'm sure you haven't noticed because you never check the account, but our revenue is also down."

"I set that account up for the children's future, and I trust you, so there's no need to check it. But I will. Napoleon said his numbers are down, so that's not surprising either."

"The largest and most troubling issue, at least for the operators, is that a couple of drug organizations have begun moving their product through the island. Being criminals, they seek other earning opportunities on the island."

"What do you plan on doing about it?"

"Long-term or short?"

"Give me the big picture first."

"Move our main operation someplace else."

"Where did you have in mind?"

"I haven't gotten that far ahead in my thinking. However, since we already have an operation there, Aruba or perhaps the Turks and Caicos are a consideration."

"Which economies are growing?"

"I've done some preliminary research, and islands, including Turks and Caicos and the Dominican Republic, are experiencing strong fiscal growth. I noted that a Saudi Fund for Development is investing in Antigua and Barbuda."

"Stay on top of that. No reason for us not to make that good Saudi money."

"No reason at all."

"You thinking about cutting our loss in the Bahamas?"

"Yes, if the trend continues."

"What about the Yellow Rose?"

"It's your house. I just live there."

"If it comes to that, sell it before the housing market crashes." Black paused. "I guess that applies to Pariso and Freeport."

"It does. This poses the question, what would you like to do with Bernadette?"

"I arrange for her to get a substantial pension, and she can return to cooking at that restaurant where Cee found her."

"She already has. I'm rarely there, so she just cleans the house and leaves. If I need her, I call, and she'll come." Jada paused. "And lately, I've been giving a good bit of thought to giving up the island life and moving back to the city."

"Really?"

"Yes, Mr. Black. I'm a New York City girl."

"That settles that," Black said, knowing that Shy wouldn't be all that happy about Jada making a move back to the city. One of the major reasons she could happily coexist with Jada was that she was in another country. "With all that said, tell me your short-term plan to resolve the operators' issues."

"Not much, actually. I have no intention of starting a war with those organizations. I will have Johnny push back gently and recommend that the operators act to defend their revenue. However, if our long-term objective is to, as you say, cut our losses, no other course of action seems appropriate."

"Agreed," Black said as his phone rang. He glanced at the display and answered. "Hello, Cassandra. Heard you and Rain are out hunting."

"Yes, Michael, we were, and our hunt was successful."

"I take it the information you got from Victor paid off?"

"It did."

"Excellent."

"So, Mr. Big Dick, I'll see you when I get home," Shy said flirtatiously.

"See you there."

"Oh, yeah, Rain said Sherman needs to talk to you, and she does too."

"Put her on the phone."

Shy handed Rain the phone. "This Rain."

"What does Sherman want to talk about?"

"He didn't say. Just that he needed to talk."

"Tell Cassandra I'm gonna stop by there and see what he wants."

"Will do."

"What about you?"

"What I need to talk about will keep until tomorrow. Is Wanda in the city?"

"Not that I know of. I offered to pick her up, but she said it would take too long and I needed to be here. She would make her own arrangements. Barbara's her girl, so I wouldn't be surprised if she shows up sometime tomorrow. Why?"

"If she's in the city, she needs to be there. Bobby too."

"This sounds serious."

"It is, but it will keep until tomorrow."

"Okay. Call me tomorrow, and wherever Bobby is, that's where we'll meet."

Chapter 10

Black ended the call with Rain and called Sherman.
"What's up, Mike?"
"How's it going, old man?"
"I need to talk to you."
"That's why I'm calling."
"You on your way?"
"In a few."
"Door will be unlocked. Come on in."
"See you in a little while."
After talking for a while longer with Jada about her long- and short-term plans for the Bahamas, William drove Black to meet with Sherman. As promised, the door was unlocked, and Black went inside.
"Louis XIII is waiting for you on the bar, Mike," Sherman said when Black entered the room. He was watching *It Happened One Night* with Clark Gable and Claudette Colbert. Black sat down and watched the movie for a while because he appreciated old movies too.
"So, what are we talking about?" Black asked, and Sherman recounted the story he shared with Rain earlier that evening.
"Whitey's had that coming for a long time." Black drained his glass. "I'm going to assume this is what Rain wants to discuss."
"Probably."
"Okay. Anything else?"

"I've thought a lot about this, and I'm gonna retire," Sherman said, and Black laughed. "Wasn't the reaction I was expecting."

"I understand, old man. You and Ester are ready to get back on the cruise circuit."

"Well, yeah," Sherman said and laughed. "I don't mean to leave you in a lurch, leaving you down a captain, but it's time. I really am getting too old for this shit."

Black got up and took Sherman's glass. He went to pour them both another drink.

"You know who you wanna pull the big chair out for?"

"Yeah."

"You gonna tell me, or do you want me to guess?" Sherman asked as Black handed him his drink and sat down.

"It's time to see if RJ can handle being captain."

Sherman laughed. "I'm sure Bobby will insist on it."

Black laughed too. "And you know this."

"I can tell you that he stepped up and handled this business with Shayla Clark. I think he can handle it, but only if he wants it."

"We will see if he wants it, won't we?"

Chapter 11

After he left Sherman's house, William drove Black to their New Rochelle house. On the way, he had a lot on his mind. Naturally, his primary thoughts were of Barbara. He was glad that she would be all right and that Shy and Rain dealt with Sanders, but Black wondered if Sanders had done the job himself and, if so, if he was alone.

Tahanee was good, very good at what she did, so the idea that one man could have entered the office, killed her, and then gone after Barbara didn't add up for him. He would talk to Barbara the first chance he got.

Then there was the matter of Shayla Clark killing Giovanni Folliero, a made man. He hadn't had any dealing with the Montanari family, but he knew the death of a made man was not going to go unanswered. The last thing they needed was another shooting war. The Family had bounced from one war to another in the past few years. The truth was, Black was tired of fighting. There were definitely times when he wished that he had stayed retired and satisfied himself with running Cuisine. But then, he would never have met his precious Cassandra.

However, the most pressing item that had the potential to cost them the most money in the long term was the issues Jada was having in the Bahamas. Although he did not doubt that Jada would make the right decision, it was still on his mind. And her moving back to New York came with its own set of challenges.

When he passed through the gate, Black was surprised to see lights were on in the living room. He entered the house and found that Michelle, M, and Joanne were still up.

"Daddy!" Michelle exclaimed when she saw him come in.

"What are y'all still doing up?"

"We got home from the hospital about an hour ago, and we've just been talking," M said, and then she and Michelle glanced in Joanne's direction.

"And Sandy left the hospital with Rain," Joanne began. Sandy was what her mother had called her all her life. She was Sandy long before she became Shy. There had been times when Black called her Sandy as well, but that was usually when someone else called her Sandy first. "So I was calling myself waiting for her to get home."

"She's not back yet?"

"Nope," Michelle said.

"I talked to her over an hour ago, and she was on her way home then."

And then, almost on cue, they heard the front door open and close, and in walked Shy.

"What y'all still doing up?"

"Waiting on you," Joanne said. "And now that you're here . . ." She stood up. "I'm going to bed."

M got up as well. "So am I."

"Good night, Grandma M, good night, Grandma Jo," Michelle said.

"Good night."

Michelle was overjoyed when her father came into the house. Barbara getting shot and Shy leaving the hospital with Rain inspired a conversation, more like a tag team lecture, that she had no desire to have with her grandmothers. If she hadn't been vacationing with her family, Michelle would have been in the office with Barbara and Tahanee and may have suffered the same fate.

Therefore, the Golden Girls had spent the last hour encouraging Michelle not to follow in Barbara's footsteps. They felt that she needed to stay focused on college, to consider getting her master's and upon graduation, taking a position in her father's legitimate business, and not becoming involved in the family business.

"Right."

Michelle intended to focus on and graduate from college and would consider a master's degree. Then she planned to work at Prestige Capital and Associates and spend time in every department so she would know every aspect of the business. But her ambition in life hadn't changed. She intended to one day succeed Rain Robinson as boss of the Family, and nothing would change that.

"What about you?" Shy asked as she followed Black upstairs to their bedroom.

"I'm gonna stay up for a while," Michelle replied and picked up the television remote.

"Okay. Good night."

"Good night, Mommy."

When Shy came into the room, she saw that her husband was getting undressed. He got up early that morning, and he was tired. He planned to take a long hot shower and go to bed. But he knew from Shy's "Mr. Big Dick" comment that she had other things on her mind.

"I'm going to shower," Black said and went into the bathroom.

"Okay."

Black turned on the water, and once it reached a comfortable temperature, he got in and allowed the hot water to wash away the stresses and pressures of the day. Shy sauntered into the bathroom where, as it always did, her breath was taken away at the sight of her husband's lean body through the glass shower door.

"God, I love that man," she said as she watched the water cause his skin to glisten.

When he turned and saw her standing there, Black watched as Shy stripped down to nothing and opened the shower door.

He took his sexy wife in his arms, and his mouth cupped hers. Shy's tongue attacked his with fury, and she could feel the river flowing between her thighs. She was always hungry for him, but tonight was different. Shy was near desperation to feel him. Black took her nipple between his lips. It sent a sensation rushing through her body. He kissed her again, nibbled her chin, and sucked her neck.

Black pinned her up against the shower wall, eased her legs open, dipped his finger inside her, and then stroked her just the way she liked it. Shy felt her body.

"That feels so good, Michael. Never stop loving me."

"Never, my love," he whispered, cupping her thick thighs and lifting her off her feet before he thrust himself into her.

Her eyes were open wide, as was her mouth, and her breath was caught in her throat. Her muscles tightened their firm grip on him as Black pushed himself deeper inside her. Shy rocked her hips, moving her body into his, and he bent his legs to pump harder.

"Fuck me, Michael."

Black felt her juices flow and gazed into her eyes. Her organism was intense and satisfying, but Shy wasn't done. She dropped to her knees and took his length into her mouth. He steadied himself against the wall and marveled at her skills.

They turned off the shower, dried each other, and rushed to the bed. He ran his hand along her body and began kissing her.

Shy rolled on her back. He spread her legs and moved in between her thighs. He entered her slowly and gently, easing his entire length inside her wetness, sliding in and out of her, and felt her body tremble. And then, all at once, Black began to move faster, and Shy quickened her pace to match his. She could feel Black expanding inside her, so she began rocking her hips furiously, pounding her body into his until she had taken it all from him. Black was in ecstasy, and so was Shy.

"You fill me up so completely, Michael."

Shy placed her hands on his legs, and with her feet on the bed, she eased her body down on him and started to move up and down effortlessly. Black arched his back and pushed himself as deep and as hard into her as he could. Shy collapsed on his chest and began slamming his hips, bringing it down hard on him. She kissed him passionately, and her head drifted back with her mouth open and eyes wide.

Chapter 12

When Black opened his eyes in the morning, he saw that Shy was dressed in a Michael Kors single-button blazer and flared pleated trousers. He rolled on his back, and after a good yawn and stretch, he sat up in bed.

"You're up early."

"I have a meeting with Pooja Rajani."

Shy still hadn't replaced Reeva Duckworth; at this point, she saw little reason to do so. Between her and Pooja, whom Shy hired away from Valencia DeVerão, they handled all of Reeva's responsibilities, and CAMB Overseas Importers was back running smoothly.

"After the meeting, I'm gonna go to the hospital to see Barbara, and then I'm coming home and getting back in bed. What about you?" she asked, hoping he would say that he'd be right there waiting for her.

"I've gotta meet Rain. She needs to talk to me and Bobby."

"Where?"

"Wherever Bobby is when Rain is ready to talk."

"Okay, then I might see you at the hospital."

"You might." Black paused. "So, what happened last night, gangster, just so I know."

Shy sat down on the edge of the bed. "Victor put us on to his girlfriend, who led us straight to him." Shy giggled. "I hit him with the car, and then we shot him."

"Overkill?"

"No. He was still moving when we shot him."

"Okay."

"What about you? How was your night?"

"Well, let me see. Sherman's retiring."

"I kinda saw that coming."

"Carmen is moving back to New York."

"Is Marcus moving with her?"

"I don't think so."

"I kinda saw that coming too. I saw the 'let's just get this over with' look on her face when she was walking down the aisle."

"And Jada is thinking about moving back."

"Why?"

"Things on the island are changing."

Shy stood up, shaking her head. "We'll talk about that when I get home. I'm already gonna be late. But you realize I prefer your exes to live in other states and other countries, so you know I'm not happy about this," she said, heading for the door in their bedroom.

"Have a nice day," Black said as the door closed behind her.

If he chose to be honest, he, too, preferred Jada to be in Nassau and for Carmen to be married and live in Atlanta. Carmen always found too many ways to get herself into trouble in New York. Regardless of whether she was happy, Carmen was definitely safer behind the anchor desk.

Meanwhile, Bobby and Pam were in the hospital room with Barbara. Pam had spoken with the twins the night before, and they were catching the first flight out of LA that morning.

Bobby looked at his daughter. His worst fears of Barbara's presence in the family business had been realized. She'd been shot, and yes, she survived and was going to be all right, but that was a combination of luck and an inexperienced shooter who didn't make sure he finished the job. He was happy to hear that Rain and Shy got Terrell Sanders, but like Black, he knew that there had to be another shooter.

"Morning, Bobby," Reverend Jones said when he entered Barbara's room. "Mrs. Ray."

"Morning, Rev."

"Good morning, Reverend," Pam said. She had been holding Barbara's hand since she came into the room.

"How's our girl?"

"The doctor said she will be fine in a few days. She just needs to rest and heal."

"Do you mind if I say a few words of prayer over her?"

"Please do, Reverend. She needs prayer," Pam said.

"But you know it's gonna be more than just a few words, Rev," Bobby said, taking Pam's hand.

"You know I like to be thorough and cover everything in prayer, Bobby," the reverend said, taking Bobby's hand.

"God, please, show us favor, and be our strength every morning and our salvation in these times of distress. By your patience in suffering, you hallowed earthly pain and gave us the example of obedience to your Father's will. Be near this family in their time of weakness and pain. Sustain them by your grace so their strength and courage will not fail. Heal your daughter, Barbara, according to your will. Lift her up for your blessings. Anoint her with strength and self-care today, tomorrow, and always. I pray all of these things in your name. Amen."

"Thank you, Reverend," Pam said.

"You're welcome, Mrs. Ray. I hope I wasn't too wordy for you, Bobby."

"About what I expected, Rev."

"And now, if you'll excuse me, I have other souls that I need to pray for this morning."

"The Lord's work is never done, right, Rev?" Bobby said.

"It continues minute by minute."

"Thank you for coming," Pam said as the reverend approached the door.

"Please call me and keep me updated."

Despite the apparent conflict between church and crime, Reverend Jones crossed that bridge and provided support to both Black and Bobby. Black was raised going to church, and M insisted on it. In fact, he was an altar boy, so when he got shot in the Bahamas, Black sought guidance from Reverend Jones. When Bobby was shot, he too sought the reverend's counsel.

It wasn't long after the reverend left the room that Pam felt Barbara squeeze her hand, and she opened her eyes.

"Mommy?"

Pam squeezed her hand tighter, and Bobby bounced out of his seat and rushed to Barbara's bedside.

"Where am I?"

"You're in the hospital, baby. You got shot," Pam informed her.

"Tahanee?"

"Tahanee didn't make it. I'm sorry," Bobby said, and tears rolled down Barbara's cheeks. "I'm going to get the nurse."

When Bobby returned with the nurse, he checked Barbara's vital signs and changed the dressing on her wounds. While he worked on Barbara, Detectives Hudson and Luna entered the room. Knowing that they needed to talk to Barbara right away and that the possibility existed that any delay in speaking to her might be complicated by lawyers and security, making it days before they got a shot at her, the detectives were waiting in their car for Barbara to regain consciousness. They had a nurse call them as soon as that happened.

The Bang, Bang, Bang 65

"Good morning, Mr. and Mrs. Ray. My name is Detective Hudson, and this is my partner, Detective Luna. We've been assigned to investigate your daughter's case. Is it all right if we speak to her now?" he asked respectfully.

Bobby looked at Barbara, and when she nodded, Hudson approached the bed while Luna hung back.

"Hello, Barbara."

"Hi, Darius."

"How are you feeling?"

"Tired and weak."

"I'm sorry. But I'm glad you're gonna be all right." Hudson paused. "Is it all right if I ask you some questions?"

"Go ahead."

"Has anybody told you about Tahanee?" Barbara nodded solemnly. "I'm sorry. I know you and Tahanee were close."

"Thank you, Darius."

"Can you tell me what happened last night?"

"We were at the office, working late as usual, and I heard Tahanee call my name, and then I heard the shot. I came out of my office and saw two men approaching me. I ran into the conference room and hid behind the table. I don't remember anything after that."

"Did you exchange gunfire with the shooters?"

"Yes."

"She has a license to carry that firearm," Bobby added quickly.

"Tell me about that, Barbara."

"When I heard the shot, I got my gun from my drawer and ran out into the hallway to see if Tahanee was all right when I saw them. So I ran to the conference and hid behind the table, and we were exchanging fire the entire time."

"Thank you, Barbara."

"So, just so I'm clear, you heard Tahanee call to you and then the gunshot. You got your gun out of your drawer and exchanged fire with them until you were behind the table, and you don't remember anything after that. Do I have that right?"

"Yes, that's right," Barbara said as Black entered the room.

"Did you get a look at them shooters?"

"No. They wore masks, so I never saw their faces."

Detective Hudson stood up. "Thank you, Barbara. If you think of anything else, please call me. And I am so sorry about Tahanee," he said, and Barbara nodded.

When Hudson turned to leave, Black was standing in front of him. "Mr. Black."

"Detective Hudson." He shook Hudson's hand. "Now, if you'll excuse me, I'd like to see about my niece," Black said, sitting beside the bed as the detectives left the room. Black watched as Bobby held the door open for Hudson and Luna and watched them walk down the hall before he spoke to Barbara.

"Hello, Barbara."

"Hi, Uncle Mike."

"How do you feel?"

"I've never been shot before, but I guess I feel like I've been shot," Barbara said with a little smile for her favorite uncle.

"You know who did this to you?"

"No, Uncle Mike, I never saw them before. But I did get a good look at them. After they shot me, they both took off their masks while they were standing over me."

"Arrogant fucks," Bobby said.

"So, you can identify them if you see them again?" Black asked.

"Yes, Uncle Mike. Those are two faces I will never forget."

"Was Sanders one of them?"

"No. I've met Sanders, and it wasn't him."

"I know what your wishes for him were, and it's been taken care of by Rain and your aunt Shy," Black informed her, and Barbara nodded.

Chapter 13

"But if Terrell Sanders wasn't one of the shooters, that means the actual shooters are still out there," Bobby said.

"We'll find them, Bob, I promise you that," Black assured him.

"In the meantime, we need to get some men to guard this room in case they try again."

"I'll take care of that," Black said as Rain entered the room.

"What's up, y'all?" Rain went to the bed and took Barbara's hand.

"Hey, Aunt Rain. I hear I owe you and Aunt Shy a debt."

"It was my pleasure to handle that."

"Thank you."

"How are you feeling?"

"I'll be fine. At least, that's what they tell me," Barbara said bravely to the boss of the Family. "But I hurt like I've never been hurt before."

"You're strong. You'll get through this, I promise." Rain chuckled. "I've been shot a bunch of times, and I'm still standing."

"But you're a bad bitch, Aunt Rain."

"And so are you. Trust me." Rain let go of Barbara's hand and turned to Black and Bobby. "I need to talk to you two."

"Let's talk outside," Black said and started for the door. Bobby and Rain followed him out.

When they left the room, Wanda and her assistant, Keisha Orr, were coming down the hallway. After hellos and hugs, Wanda had a question.

"Where are you three going?"

"We need to talk about something, and you need to hear it too," Rain said.

"Okay. Give me a minute to see Barbara first, and I'll be right out," Wanda replied.

When she came out a few minutes later, Black, Bobby, and Rain were leaning against the walls, waiting for her.

"So, what are we talking about?" Wanda asked.

"Outside," Black said and headed toward the elevator.

Bobby, Wanda, and Rain followed him out. Once they were a reasonable distance from the prying eyes and ears, Black turned to Rain.

"Go ahead, Rain."

"One of your numbers runners, Shayla Clark, killed a made man in the Montanari family."

"That is not good," Wanda said.

"No, it isn't," Rain responded and went on to explain the circumstances that led to the shooting.

"Who is this woman?" Wanda asked. "There was a time when I knew every member of this family personally. I feel so out of it."

"I know her," Bobby said.

"I know she's Eddie Clark's daughter. Used to call him 'Reaper,'" Black said, and Wanda nodded that she remembered him. "But I haven't seen her or her brother since they were kids."

"So, what do the Montanaris want?" Bobby asked.

"Her head on a spike," Rain said. "Sherman said there've been a couple of confrontations. Nothing major, no guns were drawn, but they are adamant about wanting her dead. I got her someplace safe until we decide what to do."

"We're not giving her up, are we?" Bobby asked.

"Hell no," Black said. "I'm going to talk to Angee, see if he can't arrange a sit-down with the Montanaris, see if we can't work something out."

"How soon can you make that happen?" Rain asked.

"I'm gonna try to make it happen today."

"Okay." Rain nodded. "In the meantime, I'll put everyone on notice that these fuckas are out there and not to engage them unless it's absolutely necessary."

"Right," Bobby said. "We're not trying to go to war with these crackers over this."

"No, we're not," Black said, pausing. "There's something else I need to let you know."

"What's that?" Wanda asked.

"Sherman is retiring."

"Again," Bobby said and laughed.

"He's served you well over the years," Wanda stated.

"He has." Black looked at Bobby. "As of now, RJ is acting captain of that crew," he said, and both Bobby and Wanda smiled because they had been grooming him for the role practically since birth. They felt he was the heir apparent to Rain's title as boss of the Family. She nodded but said nothing.

"I'm going to be honest with you. I've had my doubts about him," Black said, and Rain nodded because she'd also had her doubts. "Sherman has agreed to be his consigliere. But it's time to see if he can handle running the crew."

"He can handle it," Bobby said confidently and proudly. "Thank you, Mike."

"No need to thank me. He needs to step into this opportunity and prove his doubters wrong."

"He will," Wanda said.

"We'll see," Rain replied. "I'm out."

"I am too. I'm gonna try to get with Angee," Black said and walked away with Rain as Bobby and Wanda returned to the hospital.

"You sure about this?" Rain asked.

"I'm sure he deserves a chance to prove us wrong."

"Okay. But at times, RJ seems more like a businessman than committed to the business of this Family. I thought Marvin would have been a better choice to be captain."

"So did I, and his time will come." Black chuckled. "But I didn't feel like hearing Bobby's mouth, or Wanda's, for that matter, if I didn't pull the chair out for him."

"They're both gung ho about it," Rain said, laughing.

"Something else I need to make you aware of," Black said when he got to his Cadillac XT6. William opened the door. "What you got to do now?"

"Nothing pressing, why?"

"Ride with me to see Angee."

"No problem," Rain said, and they got into the SUV. She didn't have a great relationship with Angelo, but as boss of the Family, she knew she needed to.

"Things are going on in the Bahamas," Black began and told Rain what Napoleon and Jada had told him, and he laid out what Jada had in mind for the future of their very profitable Caribbean operation.

"So, we're leaving Nassau to these gangs?" Rain wanted to know.

"No. But because of what's happening, we might sell Paraiso and buy something to maintain a smaller operation."

"I see."

"One more thing."

"What's that?"

"Jada is making noises about moving back to the city."

Rain laughed. "Does that create a problem for you?"

"Not at all."

"I was talking about Shy."

"I know."

"And?"

"We'll see how that goes if and when it happens." Black took out his phone to make a call.

"Mikey!" Angelo answered. "How's it going?"

"Everything is all right, but I need to talk to you. Is it OK if me and Rain come out?"

"Shit, yeah. I ain't seen Rain in years. Come on out. I'll be here waiting for you," Angelo said.

"Thanks, Angee. We'll see you in about an hour."

When Black and Rain arrived at the mansion Angelo inherited from the former boss of the Curcio family, his uncle Big Tony Collette, they were passed through the gate by Angelo's men and escorted to the study where Angelo conducted business.

"Mikey!" Angelo said, standing with his arms raised welcomingly. Black and Angelo had been friends since they were in high school. It was Big Tony who raised them in the life they've chosen to live. "Rain! How the fuck are you?"

"I'm doing fine, Angelo. How are you?"

"I know you know the big chair comes with its own share of headaches, but I would not have it any other way."

"Tell me about it."

Angelo sat back in his chair. "Since you brought the boss along, I know you didn't come to get drunk and talk shit, so what gives, Mikey?"

"Rain," Black said, and Rain explained the situation to Angelo.

"Giovanni Folliero, that prick. Nobody's gonna miss that fuck. But he is a made guy. His uncle drives for

Nereo Bello, the boss of the Montanari family, so he was made before he deserved it. But like I said, he is a made guy, so they will want blood. I'll see if I can arrange a sit-down with you and Angiolo Marino, Bello's underboss. See if we can't come to some understanding."

"That's all I can ask for. Thank you, Angelo," Rain replied.

Chapter 14

"What's up, Pop?" RJ asked.

"I need you to come to the house tonight at ten o'clock. I need to talk to you about something. Something important," Bobby said, barely able to contain his excitement. His son was going to be made a captain that night.

Fuck that acting shit. My boy is the captain of his own crew.

"What's up?"

"Not over the phone. I'll tell you when you get here."

"I'll be there."

"Good. Be on time and come alone," Bobby said, ending the call before RJ could ask any more questions.

RJ returned his phone to his pocket, thinking that being on time and arriving alone were strange requests coming from his father. But it was his father, so he tried not to read too much into it. He left The Late Night and drove to his parents' house in Rockland County. He thought that Bobby wanting to see him was all good. He hadn't seen Venus or his son since he saw them at the hospital the night Barbara got shot, and he tried to spend some part of every day with them.

It wasn't quite ten when he arrived at the house on Wild Ginger Run. RJ entered the house, and after speaking to his mother, he went upstairs to his old room to see his family. Naturally, they were glad to see him. Venus handed him their crying baby.

"Did you find who shot Barbara and killed Tahanee?" Venus asked.

"Not yet," RJ said as his son got quiet in his father's arms.

"Then what are you doing here? Not that I'm not glad to see you."

"Pop called and said he wanted to talk to me about something."

"What?"

"He didn't say. He just said to be on time," RJ said and glanced at his watch. He handed her the baby again. "I'll be back before I leave." He kissed her and the baby and left the room on his way to the basement. When he got down there, Bobby looked at his watch.

"Good, you're early. Sit down, RJ," Bobby said, and RJ did as his father asked.

"What's up?"

"Some people in this Family think you have too much on your plate."

"What?"

"Word is that with Venus and the baby and the promotion business, you're not focused on the Family, and you're not ready to assume more responsibility."

RJ looked confused. "Where is this coming from?"

"Does it matter?" Bobby paused. "What matters is do you think that it's true?"

"No, Pop. I get done what I need to get done for the Family. The Family comes first."

"That's exactly what I wanted to hear."

"What's going on, Pop?" RJ asked as he heard footsteps coming down the stairs.

When he looked toward the steps to see who was coming, RJ saw Black.

He smiled. "What's up, Uncle Mike?"

Black said nothing, and RJ dropped the smile when he saw Rain, Wanda, and Sherman enter the basement behind Black. Especially Sherman.

He never leaves the house.

"Stand up, RJ," Rain barked once everyone was seated.

RJ stood up and wondered if he should say anything. Something was about to happen, something big; otherwise, Wanda and Sherman wouldn't be there.

"Sherman," Rain said.

"I'm retiring, RJ," Sherman said, and RJ remained silent.

"That means his crew needs a captain," Rain began. "We're looking for somebody who knows the crew and can step into Sherman's shoes and handle it." Rain paused. "Do you understand?"

"Yes, Aunt Rain, I understand," RJ said, feeling a little disappointed because he thought Rain would say that Nate Irby would be named captain. He didn't like it, but Irby had been with Sherman since the old days and was a great earner.

"As of right now, and until I say different, you are the acting captain of Sherman's crew." Black stood up. "Congratulations, RJ." He shook RJ's hand.

"Thank you, Uncle Mike."

"Don't disappoint the confidence I'm showing in you today."

"I won't, Uncle Mike."

Chapter 15

It was after two in the morning, and Pesce, an Italian restaurant in Tribeca, had closed for the night, but the bar was still open. The Four Kings, RJ, Marvin, Judah, and Baby Chris, gathered to celebrate. Marvin stood up and raised his glass.

"I would like to be the first to propose a toast." The Kings stood up and raised their glasses. "To RJ, the acting captain of his own crew."

All four drank to it.

"Fuck that 'acting' shit!" Judah shouted. "That ain't nothing but some Jedi mind trick shit Uncle Mike running on you." He went to the bar to grab another bottle of champagne. "That acting captain shit is for the old heads and the haters."

"For Irby and them," Baby Chris added.

"You're a captain, my brother. Can't nobody take that from you," Judah said and refilled everybody's glass.

RJ chuckled. "Nobody but Uncle Mike."

He thought about what Bobby had said about some members of the Family doubting whether he was ready to be a captain. Although he wondered who it was, he knew that was why he was just an "acting" captain. To RJ, it meant that he needed to prove to his doubters that he was ready for the big chair.

"And Rain. Rain could change that," Marvin said. "Probably your Pops and Aunt Wanda too."

"Fuck that shit, Money. Even though you're right," Judah laughed. When RJ was first introduced to Marvin, he was a small-time weed dealer named "Money Marv." RJ told him that if he wanted to be a part of this Family, he would need to quit dealing. Marvin stopped selling weed that same day. However, the name "Money Marv" stuck. "Fuck that shit. We here to celebrate the new captain." He raised his glass, and the others followed suit. "To RJ."

"To RJ!" Marvin and Baby Chris repeated, and they drained their glasses.

"Thank you, Judah." He popped another bottle. "I'm gonna need you to step up," RJ said, and once he had refilled their flutes, he raised his glass. "To Judah. New lieutenant of the crew."

"To Judah!" Marvin and Baby Chris repeated, and they drained their glasses again.

"Thank you, RJ. You know I'm ready to put in work for you."

When his father, Doc, was assassinated, Judah thought he should have been made captain of that crew. But when that didn't happen, he wasn't bitter. Judah kept his head down and worked to build on what his father had created—his legacy in the Family.

The first thing he did was modernize the house that the Family had operated in for years. Doc was killed outside the home. He felt the redesign would help those thoughts and memories, but it didn't. Each time he walked by the spot where Doc was killed, Judah felt the pain and the loss. Therefore, expansion was necessary.

Judah didn't have the head for business that RJ and Marvin did. Both men were running legitimate businesses. But he did know how to run strip and gambling clubs, and that's where he focused his attention. He opened three new strip clubs and separated the gambling operations from the women.

One he named Doc's, and that's where he did business. He didn't close the house because there were still the old heads who had done their gambling there for years. Now, it's referred to as Doc's House. In addition to the new spot for Doc's, Judah opened two more gambling spots, and once he saw how much money Ryder was making, he got into the live cam girl business.

"I know you're ready. You stay that way," RJ said.

"I'm gonna need something a little stronger than this champagne," Marvin said and went behind the bar. He grabbed a bottle of Chivas Regal 12. "What are you drinking, RJ?"

"Hennessy Black, Money."

As Marvin got the bottle and poured him a drink, Baby Chris went behind the bar and got a bottle of Good Fucking Bourbon whiskey. Marvin handed RJ his drink and put the bottle on the bar.

"Get me a glass while you back there, Money," Judah requested. When Marvin handed him the glass, he poured himself a glass of Hennessy Black.

"What's your first official act as acting captain gonna be?" Marvin asked.

"Renovate Mama's and get the gambling back up and running."

After Big Chet French robbed the gambling room at Mama's Country Kitchen, Sherman had closed the gambling there.

"Then I'm gonna open some new gambling spots." RJ laughed. "I might even get into the restaurant business like you."

"Plenty of money in food," Marvin said.

Where RJ owned gambling and dance clubs in addition to his very successful promotion business, all of Marvin's businesses were legit. He owned a construction company, two restaurants, Pesce Tribeca, a Mediterranean restaurant, Trikala Greek Taverna, Healthy Lifestyle fitness center, and The Power Punch Gym. He also managed welterweight contender Alex "The Bronx Bomber" Benton. Marvin and Baby Chris were Jackie's enforcers, and they functioned as her lieutenants but didn't carry the title. He had impressed the right people in that position, and it was a sure thing that one day, he would be a captain.

"I wanna make an announcement," Marvin said, refilling and then raising his glass. "BC is opening his first business next month."

"Congratulations," both RJ and Judah said, and they drank to it.

"What you gonna open?" Judah asked.

"Big nightclub. With gambling, of course." BC chuckled.

"What you gonna call it, BC?" RJ asked.

"Don't know yet. But I'm hoping to get The Regulators for the opening night."

"You got them." RJ laughed. "And I'll only charge you The Four Kings' price."

"Four Kings!" all four men cheered and drank to it.

"Thank you, RJ," Baby Chris said.

"No problem," RJ replied.

Although he was the second generation in the Family like the other Kings, Baby Chris wasn't a legacy. His father wasn't a captain or a founding member; his father was Babyface Arcus, a soldier and bank robber. Therefore, he had no delusions about being anointed captain due to his lack of legacy status. If it happened, it would be because he had put in the work and earned it as he had earned his place in this exclusive club.

Marvin looked at RJ. "I was gonna ask your pops to sell me Impressions."

"That would be a good move for you, Money," RJ said.

Although Impressions had been a Family business for years, it was, and had always been, completely legitimate. To the Family, this meant there was no gambling, and no one ran their business out of there. Therefore, Impressions didn't fall under any of the established captain's jurisdictions. And that was what made it attractive to Marvin.

"It would have been, but I had to back away from it," Marvin said and drained his glass.

"How come?" RJ asked.

"I needed that money for something else."

"I'll back you, Money," Baby Chris said. "If you're still interested."

"You're serious?"

"Yeah, I'm serious."

"You got that kind of money, BC?" Judah asked.

"Shit yeah, that nigga got it." Marvin laughed. "Big Bank Payton got his back."

"She does. And we're looking for investments to make."

Payton Cummings was a very successful hedge fund manager who made more money than she could have ever imagined.

"Must be nice," Judah commented.

"Trust me, it is," Baby Chris said.

"There is something I need to make you all aware of." RJ looked at Marvin and Baby Chris. "Jackie will probably talk to the two of you about it."

"What's up?" Baby Chris asked.

"Do you know a runner named Shayla Clark?"

Baby Chris smiled and nodded. "I know her. *Very* well," he said because he fucked her.

"Me too," Marvin said because he had fucked her as well.

More than once.

RJ laughed. "By the way, Money," he began but still laughed, "I forgot to tell you that I saw Sataria a couple of days ago, and she looked good. She said to tell you hello and that she still loves you."

"Fuck that," Marvin shot and then poured himself another drink. "If you see her fine ass again, you tell her for me that I said that I love her too. But I will never trust her black widow ass ever again in life."

Although she claimed that she never told them to do it, after talking to Sataria, men had killed her first husband, and Marvin killed her second husband.

"Fuck that."

"Damn right, Money," Judah said. "Because eventually, she'd get tired of you fuckin' Joslin Braxton, and she'd get somebody to kill you."

"Exactly. So, fuck that. Fuck Sataria's black widow ass and that dumb-ass love shit," Marvin said.

"Which reminds me," RJ began. "Judah."

"'Sup?"

"What's up with you and Edwina?"

"Huh?"

"You heard me, nigga. What's up with you and Edwina?"

"Ain't nothing up. We're just friends. We grew up together. We've been tight since we were kids," Judah said in his defense.

"Right. I was a kid right along with the two of you. I grew up with her too, and she doesn't look at me the way she looks at you." RJ laughed. "And she doesn't get all girly when she's around me the way she does when she gets around you."

"I've noticed that too," Marvin said. "What's up with that?"

"Okay, okay." Judah smiled. "Me and her been involved for a while."

"Try *years*," RJ said.

"Okay, RJ, damn. Me and her been together for *years*. But she's very private and doesn't want the Family in her business."

"That's why when you'd show up at fights and shit with some dancer from the club, I never ask you anything about them because I know better."

"You're right. They just be showpieces," Judah admitted.

"Anyway," RJ said with a chuckle, "Shayla killed Bryon White and a made guy named Giovanni Folliero. He with the Montanari family."

"That's not good," Marvin said.

"Not good at all," Baby Chris cosigned.

"I'm gonna need you to start beefing up our muscle, Judah. I got a feeling these Montanari people will go to the mattresses over this."

"On it," Judah said.

"Killing a made guy," Marvin began. "Damn right, they're going to the mattresses."

RJ returned to the bar to refresh his drink. "Rain's got her stashed somewhere for now, but it's coming."

"Pour me one while you're at it, RJ."

"Might as well make it two," Baby Chris said.

RJ poured his own drink. "Who do I look like? The fuckin' maid or somebody? I just made captain. Shiiit, y'all should be pouring *my* drinks."

"Why you gotta be like that, RJ?" Baby Chris said as he dragged himself out of his seat and grabbed the bottle of Good Fucking Bourbon whiskey.

"Pour me one while you at it, BC," Judah said, refusing to move.

"Who do I look like? The fuckin' maid up in here?" Baby Chris laughed and handed Judah the bottle of Hennessy Black.

"Thank you, BC." He pointed at RJ. "That's what's wrong with Black people, RJ. Y'all never wanna do nothing for nobody," Judah said as he poured himself a drink.

"That's cool, RJ. This is your night." Baby Chris poured him another drink. "If facedown drunk is what you wanna be, facedown drunk it is," Baby Chris said, and The Kings laughed with him. But not RJ. He seemed to be in deep thought.

"Yo, RJ. What's wrong with you?"

"Nothing's wrong, Money. I was just thinking about how lucky I am, that's all. To have good friends like y'all."

"You ain't about to get all misty on us, are you, RJ?" Baby Chris asked.

"I hope not," Judah said and lit a blunt. "'Cause if you are, I'm out. I hate seeing men cry."

"Nobody's gonna be doing any damn crying. Just pass the blunt and pour me another drink. Damn, all I was saying is it's not easy to find real friends. That's all. But you muthafuckas think I'm about to get weak and shit."

"I know what you're saying. I feel the same way, and quiet as it's kept, those two do too. I love you, niggas. Y'all are like brothers to me, and I will fuck up the first one who calls me weak," Marvin said.

"Lighten up, Money," Judah responded. "You're too intense. It's all that junk food you eat. You need to eat more fresh fruit and vegetables."

"Look, the only veggie I need more of is that blunt, so pass it over," Marvin said, taking the blunt from Baby Chris and taking a long drag. "See, I'm more relaxed already."

He passed the blunt to RJ and stood up. He hit the blunt and raised his glass. When he did, the others stood and raised their glasses as well.

"To us!"

"Four Kings for life." they all said and drank to it.

Chapter 16

Barbara had just drifted off to sleep at Saint Barnabas Hospital in the morning. She hadn't gotten much sleep the night before. She couldn't get comfortable, and the lights from the hallway shone brightly into the room. When she finally fell asleep, a nurse who came to draw blood woke her. There was a light tapping on the door. Barbara opened her eyes as the door slowly opened.

"Hey, Barbie," Jolina said, entering the room with Kayla.

Barbara yawned. "Hey, y'all."

"I'm sorry. Did we wake you?" Kayla asked.

"Yes, but it's all right. I'm glad to see you," Barbara said because she got lonely after her parents, Venus, and her nephew left the night before.

"How are you feeling?" Kayla asked.

"Tired, sore." Barbara laughed lightly, but it hurt. "Like I got shot."

"I'm just glad you're all right."

"Me too," Jolina said as Destiny came into the room.

"I heard the doctor tell my father that if you hadn't got there and called for the ambulance when you did, I probably would have bled out. Thank you, Jolina. You saved my life."

"Good thing I forgot my phone," Jolina said and thought about Tahanee. "I'm sorry I didn't get there in time to help Tahanee." She also believed that had she gotten there any sooner, she might have suffered the same fate.

"What happened, Jolina?" Barbara asked.

"Like I said, when I realized I forgot my phone, I returned for it. When I arrived, I saw Tahanee and went looking for you."

"You're a hero," Destiny said.

"All I did was call 911," she said modestly.

"And that's all it took to save Barbara's life," Kayla replied.

"Do you know who did it?" Destiny asked.

"No, I don't. I've never seen them before. But I did get a good look at them. After they shot me, they came and stood over me. But instead of putting two in my head to make sure I was dead, these two amateurs took off their masks."

"Then you can identify them?" Kayla asked.

"I can, but I didn't tell the police that." Barbara looked at Jolina and smiled. "I talked to Darius. He's on the case."

"I know. I talked to him too."

"And?" Destiny asked excitedly.

"And I told him what I saw." She paused. "He was all business, and so was I."

"Okay, all business," Destiny said, giggling.

Jolina smiled and dropped her head a little. "Okay, I admit it was good to see him. But he had a job to do: finding and locking up whoever shot Barbie. That was much more important."

Kayla giggled. "Whatever, Jolina."

"Okay, so he did look good. So good I wanted to strip him down and ride that dick like a wild cowgirl in heat, but . . ." Jolina paused. "However, that was neither the time nor the place."

"When has doing the appropriate thing ever stopped you?" Destiny asked.

"When Barbie gets shot, and I gotta talk to the cops." Then she lied to her girls. "It's over between us. He made that quite clear. He's a cop, I'm a criminal, and he can't be in a relationship with a criminal. I'm over it." There was no need to tell them that she and Hudson had come to an understanding about the future of their relationship. "End of story. Can we move on now?"

"He did look good," Destiny said.

"*Real* good," Kayla cosigned.

"Y'all leave Jolina alone," Barbara said.

"Thank you, Barbie. When are they going to let you go home?" Jolina asked quickly to change the subject.

"The doctor said not for at least another couple of days. He said I lost a lot of blood, and my hemoglobin levels are low, so they wanna keep me here to get those levels back up and for observation," Barbara explained as someone tapped on the door. All eyes turned toward the door as it opened, and Michelle stepped in.

"Hey, Michelle," they said almost in unison.

"Hey, y'all," Michelle replied, approaching the bed.

"That's a cute outfit," Kayla said of the ivory Favorite Daughter satin Juniper duster and low Favorite pants.

"Thank you," Michelle said. "How are you, Barbara?"

"I've been better. But they tell me I'm gonna be fine."

"That's good to hear. I was so worried when Daddy got the call. Next thing you know, we're on the jet. But you're gonna be all right, right?"

"Yes, Michelle, I'm going to be fine," Barbara assured her.

"Must be nice to have a jet," Destiny said.

"You ever get to fly it?" Kayla asked.

"I've sat in the pilot's seat while we were in flight and held on to the control wheel while Jake, our pilot, pointed stuff out on the primary flight display. But I've never taken off or landed."

"The important stuff," Kayla said.

"Still, must be nice," Destiny said again.

"It is."

"How was your trip?" Barbara asked.

"Super boring. I mean, there was a lot to do, but the other people my age were all white, and the girls were not friendly and maybe a bit racist."

"What about the boys?" Jolina asked.

"Immature and overanxious," Michelle said, and everybody laughed. "So, I ended up spending a lot of time alone or hanging out with my mother."

"How is Aunt Shy?"

"She's fine. At work."

Barbara knew that she wanted to thank Shy for what she'd done, but expressing that now would lead to a discussion about Terrell Sanders and Mason Grant, and she'd already decided to remain silent on the subject. She would thank Shy when she saw her, but right then, something else was on Barbara's mind, which was a bit more critical.

"I need to talk to Michelle," Barbara said.

"You need the room?" Jolina asked.

"Yes."

"Okay," she said as Destiny and Kayla moved toward the door. "We'll be right outside."

Once the door closed, Michelle sat in the seat next to the bed.

"What did you want to talk to me about?"

"I need you to do something for me."

"What's that?"

"We have a lot of things going on, and I need you to step up and run things for me while I'm gone."

"Run things?" Michelle questioned. "Just so I'm clear about what we're talking about, run what things?"

"The business. My business." Barbara laughed. "What things did you think I was talking about?"

"That's why I asked."

"You know we're getting ready to close on the properties for condo conversion and the new club. I don't wanna cancel, so I need you to take those meetings for me."

"You're serious?" a wide-eyed Michelle asked.

"Yes, Michelle, I'm serious."

"I don't know, Barbara," Michelle said modestly, but she was excited. This wasn't what she was expecting when she woke up that morning. It was the opportunity she'd been waiting for all her life.

A chance.

This was the first real step in her progression to one day succeed Rain Robinson and become the boss of the Family.

"Come on, Michelle. You were at all the meetings. You know the specifications and the people. You can handle this. I have confidence in you. And I am just a phone call away. And Jolina will be there to help you. Can I count on you?"

"Yes, Barbara. Whatever you need me to do."

"Great." Barbara paused. "One day, you and me are gonna run this Family. Well, you more than me, and I need you to be ready."

"I'm ready."

"That's my girl."

"What about the other side of the house?"

"What about it?"

Michelle paused and tentatively asked, "Am I running that too?"

"Michelle," Barbara began, "you are me until I return. The House, Flow, the gambling, all of it." Barbara paused. "You are the boss of this crew."

"Thank you, Barbara."

"Don't thank me yet. The shit ain't gonna be easy. Niggas are gonna give you shit and not follow your orders, but you can handle it."

"Okay, Barbara. I got you."

"Thank you, Michelle. Now, I owe you *and* your mother."

"Owe my mother for what?"

"Oh. You don't know?" Barbara paused and thought about it. "Maybe I shouldn't have said anything."

"Oh, but no, Barbara. We're not doing that. Not today. You gotta tell me."

Barbara giggled. "Okay, okay. The man who sent the guys to kill me was named Terrell Sanders."

"Why did he send men to kill you?"

Barbara exhaled. "Not many people know this, but I was having an affair with Mason Grant."

"Wait, what?"

"You heard what I said."

"Mason Grant? The *actor*, Mason Grant?" Michelle asked, not really believing what she was hearing.

"Yes, Michelle. The actor, Mason Grant. Anyway, when I found out that Terrell was responsible for his death along with Willard Bellamy, I sent Axe and Press to kill him, but he got away."

"And he sent men to retaliate."

"Yes. Last night, your mother and Aunt Rain hunted Sanders down and killed him."

Michelle played it off. "She didn't have a chance to tell me. The Golden Girls were still up when she got home, and she went to work early," she said, knowing Shy wouldn't have told her even if she were alone.

Barbara laughed. "Aunt Shy is my role model. Gangster by night, businesswoman by day."

"Yeah." Michelle laughed. "She's my role model too." *And I'm gonna start acting like she is.*

"What I just told you about me and Mason Grant stays between us."

"About you and who? Did you say something that I missed?" Michelle said to her cousin, smiling.

"Good, now, go get the ladies, and we'll break it to them," Barbara said, and Michelle went to the door to let Destiny, Kayla, and Jolina back into the room. While waiting in the hallway, they had wondered what Barbara and Michelle were discussing. But as they filed back into the room, they were not expecting what they were about to hear.

"Until I get my strength back, Michelle will be running the crew," Barbara announced to her girls.

"What?" Destiny asked. With Tahanee gone, she thought Barbara would tap her for that responsibility. She and Barbara were the very best of friends while they were in high school. That all changed when Tahanee came along, and as a consequence of her job protecting Barbara and Destiny's relationship with Bishop and their loan shark business, she and Barbara drifted apart. But now, she and Bishop had broken up, and she hoped she and Barbara could return to where they were. However, it seemed like she was getting closer to Michelle instead. She was jealous, but Destiny understood that they were cousins and this was business.

"Something wrong, Dest?" Barbara asked.

"Not at all. Just surprised, that's all." Destiny turned to Michelle. "Congratulations."

"Thank you, Destiny."

"I expect all of you to do whatever you need to do to make this work. Especially you, Jolina. Michelle is gonna take those meetings to close on the properties we've been looking at, so I need you to support her as if she were me."

"You got it, Barbie. And congratulations, Michelle," Jolina said.

"Congratulations," Kayla said and turned to Jolina. "Pencil me in for the first available. There's something I need to talk to you about the expansion of our clothing line. Barbara's been putting me off."

"I have," Barbara said. She was too busy involving herself in Carmen Taylor's investigation of Mason Grant's murder to be thinking about the expansion of their clothing line. "Make that a priority, Michelle."

"I'll be in the office in the morning," Michelle said calmly, but on the inside, fireworks were going off, the marching band was playing, and she was dancing a celebratory dance.

Barbara picked up the hospital phone and made a call.

"Who is this?" Axe asked when he answered.

"It's Barbara. I'm calling on the hospital phone."

"How you doing? They say the bullet went straight through."

"It did. The doctor says I'll be up and around in a few weeks."

"Glad to hear it. And if you need anything, you know I got you, right?"

"Always my loyal soldier."

"Always."

"Like I said, I'm gonna be laid up recovering for a while, and Michelle will be in charge until I get back."

"Understood."

"I need you to protect my cousin and make it clear to everyone that her orders are to be followed," Barbara said, thinking back to days when she first took over the crew, and nobody respected her. She had to make an example of some people to prove she was to be taken seriously and not seen as Bobby's little girl. It would be the same for Michelle, only her father was Mike Black, the boss of the Family, and that carried more weight.

"I'll make sure everybody knows the deal, and I will give my life to protect her," Axe promised.

"I expected no less." Barbara ended her call with Axe. "It's settled."

Chapter 17

Axe and Press walked into Norte el Soul and looked around. They had come there looking for Alicia Hall in the hope that she might be able to lead them to Terrell Sanders' shooter. They walked up to the bar and had a seat. The bartender dropped bar napkins in front of them.

"What can I get for you, gentlemen?"

"A couple of your top-shelf scotch whiskies on the rocks," Axe said.

"Johnnie Walker Blue Label all right?"

"Run 'em," Axe said.

While the bartender went to make their drinks, Axe and Press looked around Norte el Soul.

"Which one do you think is her?" Press asked. They were told that Alicia Hall was attractive, slim, well dressed, and wore too much makeup. Axe looked at the women who were in the club. Half of them fit that description.

"Shit, ain't no telling." He scanned the club again. "My money's on the one in the red dress with spaghetti straps."

Press pointed. "I say it's her. The one in the black shoulderless dress that's sitting over there by herself."

"For how much?"

"Hundred," Press replied as the bartender returned with their drinks. "And the drinks."

Axe dug in his pocket and peeled off a couple of hundred-dollar bills. He put one on the bar in front of the bartender. "We're looking for Alicia Hall. She here?" he asked.

"Alicia—" The bartender picked up the money and looked around Norte el Soul. "Alicia, I saw her in here earlier," he said as he made change.

"Keep the change," Axe said, and the bartender pointed to a woman in an Isabel Marant minidress and, of course, way too much makeup.

He put the money in his pocket. "That's her," he said immediately, "sitting at that table by herself."

"Shit," Axe said, and Press held out his hand.

"Pay up," he said, laughing, and Axe slapped the hundred in his hand.

"Let's go," Axe said, and he and Press walked over and stood in front of the table. Alicia Hall looked up and smiled.

"What can I do for you, gentlemen?"

"Mind if we sit?" Press asked.

"That depends on what you want."

"Information," Press said.

Alicia Hall extended her hand gracefully so they could sit down.

"You know what they say?"

"What's that?" Axe asked.

"All information comes with a price," Alicia said, smiling.

Press pulled a roll of bills from his pocket. "You got information; I got money."

"Then we can do business."

Press put a hundred on the table but kept his hand on it. "You know Terrell Sanders?"

"I do."

"We're looking for who he would send to do his dirty work," Axe said, and Press removed his hand from the money.

Alicia looked at the bill on the table and then looked at Press with no smile on her face. Axe and Press glanced at each other. Press dropped another hundred-dollar bill on the table.

Alicia picked up the money. "You're looking for Jeremy Irvin, Corey Bawden, and their crew."

"Where do we find them?" Press asked.

Alicia smiled and tipped her head to one side before looking at the table. Press shook his head and peeled off another hundred. She picked up the bill and told them where they could be found.

On the way to the warehouse, where Alicia told them they would find Irvin, Bawden, and their crew, Press took out his phone and made a call.

"Who you calling?" Axe asked.

"Angel and Bowie. You heard what gobble-dollar said. There could be eight or ten guys in there. Fuckin' right, I'm calling them."

"I was gonna check it out before I called for help. But you're right. No point taking chances or wasting time, for that matter."

"Hey, handsome," Angel answered.

"Hey, Angel. What you and Bowie doing right now?"

"Who says I'm with Bowie?"

"You're always with that nigga. Fine as you are, he don't let you out of his sight."

"You're right. He's right here, and no, he don't like to let me out of his sight."

"So, what y'all into?"

"Nothing. You need us to meet you somewhere?"

"I do," Press said and gave Angel the address to the warehouse.

"We'll see you there," Angel said, ending the call.

As soon as they reached the warehouse and got to the door, one man stepped out armed with a semiautomatic weapon, took aim, and opened fire at them. As the gunman sprayed the area with shells, Axe, Press, Angel, and Bowie immediately sought better cover.

"Bitch told them we were coming," Press said.

"Yeah," Axe shouted. "And I'ma put a bullet in her brain."

Once they made it to cover, Press raised his weapon and shot the shooter in the head. When he went down, the four emerged from their cover and started toward the door again, but another man came out of the building and began firing. They were forced to seek cover once more.

"I'll go around that way, see if I can get a clear shot at him," Axe shouted and looked at Bowie. "Cover me!"

Press, Angel, and Bowie opened fire when Axe ran off to give him cover.

"We need to spread out," Angel shouted as another gunman began firing from a window. "We're fish in a barrel here."

Bowie moved out and stayed low as he ran to get a better angle on the shooter in the window. When he was in position, Axe rose, fired, and hit the man at the door, taking him out with a shot in the chest. However, he kept firing wildly as he stumbled forward and fell to the ground.

"Damn," Press said as bullets rained over his and Angel's heads.

When Bowie reached better cover, he saw Angel and Press pinned down and taking heavy fire. Bowie aimed his weapon and opened fire, hitting the gunmen in the window.

That gave Press and Angel the time to get to their feet and come out from cover.

Press and Angel ran toward the door and went in with their weapons blasting. Angel immediately had to retreat and run for cover as two more men with automatic weapons began firing at her. She dove to the floor and covered her head.

Press went in the opposite direction and returned fire at them as Axe and Bowie entered the warehouse and opened fire. It sent the shooters rushing to take cover. Once they reached better cover, the two shooters broke out heavier weapons and sprayed the area with bullets.

Axe dove for the ground, and Bowie ran for cover behind a pillar. Angel crawled along the floor to reach a spot where she could stand. When she got to a better place, Angel saw that the two shooters had separated and opened up on Bowie, trying to get him in the crossfire. Angel fired a couple of shots as Bowie moved to cover.

With their gunfire now focused on Angel, Axe kept moving to the rear of the warehouse and tried to get behind them. As the shooters continued firing at Angel, Axe quietly moved in behind one of them and began firing. When he did, Angel bounced up and started firing. They had them in the crossfire, and the shooters went down.

With only one shooter remaining, Angel and Axe concentrated their fire on him. He kept firing until his weapon was empty, but before he could get to his handgun, Angel stepped out and took him down with one shot to the head. Axe walked over to the one she killed, stood over him, and put two into his chest.

"Where's Bowie and Press?" Angel asked as shots rang out from another area of the warehouse.

Axe pointed in the direction of the shooting. "Let's go find them." He and Angel ran toward the action.

While Bowie and Press were exchanging fire with the two shooters, Axe and Angel kept moving and were fired upon. Once again, they separated and took cover. Angel moved slowly and quietly along the wall as a man ran at Axe, firing his weapon. She quickly found cover and fired at him. He took cover but kept firing at Axe until his gun was empty, but when he stopped to reload a fresh clip, Angel hit him with two shots to the chest. The gunman dropped his weapon and went down. Press came out from cover and shot another shooter in the back as he ran for cover.

Two shooters kept firing at Bowie and Press. Press went for his second gun and returned fire. One of his shots hit a gunman, and the impact took him off his feet. He hit the ground hard.

Bowie crawled to cover while the remaining gunman kept firing and walking boldly toward him. Angel, Axe, and Press all took aim and fired at the last shooter. A barrage of bullets hit him, and he fell over face-first to the ground.

As the echo of gunfire faded, Angel, Axe, and Press reloaded their weapons and walked toward Bowie. Press held out his hand, and Bowie got to his feet.

"Thanks."

The four looked around at the carnage and destruction they brought down on Terrell Sanders's men.

"I wonder if any of them are Jeremy Irvin or Corey Bawden?" Press questioned as they headed for the door.

"Doesn't matter. Mr. Black said to kill anybody that's down with him," Axe said.

Chapter 18

Marvin looked out of the window of Black's Cessna as the jet touched down in Las Vegas for a 9:00 a.m. meeting at the Red Rock Casino, Resort and Spa with Joe Pascone. At his feet was a briefcase containing one million dollars. Marvin was tired from not getting a lot of sleep the night before. He and Baby Chris had gotten a tip that some people who were loyal to Terrell Sanders could be found at a house in Queens and that they may have been the ones who shot Barbara and killed Tahanee.

When they arrived at the house in Queens, four men were standing outside, drinking beer. Marvin and Baby Chris got out of the car and started toward the house. All three dropped their bottles and drew their weapons.

"What you niggas want?" one shouted.

"To talk."

"Talking is for bitches," he shouted, and the shooting started.

He fired a few shots and then ran up on the porch. Marvin and Baby Chris drew their weapons and started shooting back as they took cover behind their car.

"Was it something I said?" Marvin joked as bullets bounced off the vehicle.

"Naw. These niggas just crazy," Baby Chris said. "What you wanna do?"

A man was standing in a doorway, firing shots at them. Marvin stood and fired twice. Both hit him in the head as he returned to cover.

"When they stop to reload, you go take the one on the left."

"Got you."

When there was a lull in the shooting, Baby Chris came up firing and hit one of the men with a head shot. At that moment, the one on the porch ran down the street, firing.

"I got him!" Marvin yelled and went after him. The man continued firing as he ran. Marvin fired a couple of shots at him, and then he stopped. He took careful aim, fired one shot, and hit the runner in the leg. He stumbled and went down hard. Marvin slowly walked up to him, stood over him, and shot him in the head at point-blank range.

Baby Chris circled around the other side of the car, fired twice, and hit his man with both shots.

It was after three in the morning when Baby Chris drove away from the scene and after four when he dropped Marvin off at his house. He was supposed to take Black to the airport for the flight to Vegas at five. He got in the shower, changed clothes, and headed for the airport.

"Rough night?" Black asked when Marvin boarded the Cessna and took a seat. After telling Black about his night, he fell asleep and woke up somewhere over Colorado.

Now that they were on the ground, they exited the aircraft. Black and Marvin were taken by limousine to the Red Rock Casino, arriving at 8:45 a.m., Las Vegas time. Once in the hotel, they went to the Onyx Bar, where they were to meet Carlo DeSalice, a longtime friend of Black and Angelo Collette. Carlo was into a little bit of everything, but his Vegas connections were why Black reached out to him.

"Mikey!" Carlo shouted from the bar when Black and Marvin arrived.

"Carlo." Black shook his hand. "How's it going?"

"You know me, Mikey, making moves and money."

"Carlo, this is my nephew, Marvin Simmons. Marvin, this is my good friend, Carlo DeSalice."

"This is Nick's son, right?" They shook hands. "I hear good things."

"Good to meet you," Marvin said.

"Did you bring it?"

Marvin held up the briefcase. "Right here."

"Good. Good deal." Carlo looked at his watch. "We need to start making our way up there."

"Let's go," Black said, and he and Marvin followed Carlo out of the bar to the elevators.

"How's this gonna go?" Marvin asked.

"Simple. We go in, you hand them the case, they count it, and we're out. Simple." Carlo laughed. "It's the handing over the case with a million dollars that's fuckin' with you. I get it. But that's it."

As they rode up in the elevator, Marvin thought about the call he got one morning from Black.

"You got half a million dollars?" Black asked.

"No, but I can get it. What do I need a half million for?"

"You actually need a million, but I'll cover the other half."

It took him a couple of days because he was planning to use the money he had to make Bobby an offer to buy Impressions, but Marvin got the money together, and now they were in Vegas.

Carlo knocked on the door.

"Who is it?"

"Carlo DeSalice."

The door cracked open, and the three men walked into the suite. Two heavily armed men stood around a short, balding man, and three naked women.

"Carlo!" Joe Pascone shouted when he came out of the bedroom wearing a hotel robe. He was a big man with a big belly, curly salt-and-pepper hair, and a thick mustache.

"Big Joe, how's it hanging?" Carlo turned to Black. "My associate, Mike Black, and his nephew, Marvin Simmons."

"Did you bring it?" Joe asked.

Marvin handed Big Joe the case. He walked to the table with it and gave it to the short, balding man. There was a bill counter on the table. While Black, Marvin, and Carlo stood and watched, the man sat down, opened the case, and ran the bills through the machine. For his part, Big Joe sat on the couch where one of the women had eased her hand under the robe.

"It's all here."

Big Joe moved the woman's hand away and stood up. "Pleasure doing business with you, gentlemen," he said. "Doris here will show you out."

Marvin looked at Black, and when he nodded, they followed Doris to the door.

"That's it?" Marvin questioned. "We hand him a million dollars, and all we get is a 'pleasure doing business with you, gentlemen'?"

Carlo laughed. "Yeah," he said as the elevator arrived, and they got on.

"Like I told you, it's an investment in your future," Black said.

Marvin exhaled. "If you say so, Uncle Mike."

"I know this is what people say before the world goes to shit. But trust me, it will all work out in the end."

Chapter 19

It was just after noon on the East Coast, and Shy was at work at CAMB Overseas Importers. She was thinking about where she wanted to go for lunch, Mamma Francesca restaurant or The Sweet Potatoes restaurant, when her assistant, Elise, told her that Elaine Cargil, President of the Association of Black Businesses, was holding on line two.

"Thank you, Elise." Shy picked up line two. "Cassandra Black."

"Hello, Cassandra. It's Elaine Cargil. How are you doing today?"

"I'm fine, Elaine. I'm a little tired. I didn't get much sleep last night," she admitted because she was out hunting with Rain Robinson. "How are you?"

"I'm good, Cassandra. I'm not going to take up a lot of your time. I'm not sure if Mike mentioned that I will run for an open Senate seat."

"He did. And anything that I can do to help, all you have to do is ask."

"Thank you, Cassandra. I'm glad to hear you say that because I was going to ask you to come and work on the campaign." Elaine laughed lightly. "Not that I think I have a Black girl's chance at a Ku Klux Klan rally of winning. But I want to highlight women's issues and the issues important to people of color and the less fortunate."

"All important issues need to be highlighted. Of course, you can count on me to help in any way I can."

"Thank you, Cassandra. I'm planning a fundraiser in a couple of weeks. If your work schedule permits, I'd like you to be on the planning committee."

"Let's get together later in the week and talk about it over lunch," Shy suggested.

"Sounds good. We'll talk soon. I'll let you get back to work," Elaine said, and after they exchanged pleasantries, Shy ended the call. She sat back in her chair and thought about herself. Shy, the ex-drug dealer with a healthy body count, working on a political campaign. . . .

You've come a long way, girl, she thought, feeling pretty pleased with herself.

Meanwhile, something was going on in the lobby that would change Shy's mood. A woman walked in wearing a rose Valentino Garavani midi dress with Giambattista Valli silk strappy sandals. She was carrying a small top-handle alligator bag made by Stalvey.

She stopped when she stepped inside and removed her Celine sunglasses with crystals. She looked around at the few people waiting in the lobby and then at the receptionist, Vandy Henderson, before walking to the counter.

Vandy posted her greeting smile because that was her job, but on the inside, she was thinking, *This bitch got nerve.*

"Welcome to Prestige Capital and Associates. How can I help you today?"

"Mrs. Susan Beason, to see Erykah Morgan, please."

"Do you have an appointment with Ms. Morgan today?"

"No, unfortunately, I do not. I was just hoping she was available to speak with me."

"I understand. If you wouldn't mind having a seat, I will see if Ms. Morgan is available to speak with you."

"Thank you. I promise not to take up a lot of her time," Susan said and went to sit down.

Vandy waited until Susan was seated before she made the call. However, instead of calling Erykah, Vandy called Shy's direct line.

"Cassandra Black."

"Good afternoon, Mrs. Black. It's Vandy."

"Yes, Vandy. What can I do for you?" Shy answered.

"I'm sorry to bother you, Mrs. Black. But Susan Beason is in the lobby, dressed up to 'beat the dance,' as my sainted grandmother used to say."

"What does she want?" Shy asked as her eyes narrowed, and her blood began to boil.

"She asked to speak to Erykah."

"Did you call her?"

"No, ma'am. I called you."

"Don't bother calling her. I'll take care of this myself. Have security meet me in the lobby, please."

"Yes, ma'am," Vandy said, disconnecting her call with Shy and happily calling security.

Shy was fuming when she dug her cell phone out of her purse and called Black.

"Hello, my love. How's your day going?" Black asked, happy to hear from his wife.

"Where are you?"

"In Vegas with Marvin. Why?"

"Then maybe you can tell me why Susan Beason is in the lobby."

"I have no idea what she's doing there. I haven't seen or talked to her since I saw her at Patrick's office that day I told you about."

"And yet, here she is. In my lobby, Michael," Shy blasted away.

"Did she say what she wanted?"

"She asked for Erykah, but you and I both know she's here looking for *you*, Michael."

"Erykah will handle her."

"No, Michael. I told you that if you didn't stop her, *I* would," Shy said, ending the call.

"Cassandra, wait," Black said to dead air.

Shy opened her desk drawer and thought seriously about getting her gun. But this was her place of business, and she needed to be an example. Not the one that caused the drama in the lobby that everybody in the building would be talking about for weeks. Shy closed her drawer and left her office on the way to the lobby. When she arrived, she stopped and looked at Susan.

Dressed up to beat the dance. I'm gonna have to ask Vandy about the origin of that expression, she thought as security approached her.

"What can we do for you, Mrs. Black?" one of the four security personnel who responded to Vandy's call asked.

"Follow me." Shy walked up and stood over Susan.

"Oh, hello, Mrs. Black. I was just—" Susan began, but Shy cut her off before she could finish her made-up excuse for being there.

"Escort this woman off the property and arrest her for trespassing if she returns," Shy said calmly. Then she turned around to go to her office to make another call.

"Wait a minute," Susan protested.

"Please stand up so we can escort you off the property, ma'am."

Susan stood up in a huff and stormed out of the lobby. Security followed her to her car. They wrote down the make, model, and license plate number, while another took pictures of the car with his cell phone. Susan drove away, thinking this was one of the most humiliating moments of her life. It made her think that maybe she should give up this foolish quest, finalize her divorce, and find a man of her own.

But it really was far too late for that.

Chapter 20

Late in the evening, former FBI agent-turned-Defense Department operative Nicole Maddox arrived at the real estate office. She put the car in park, and since it was dark, she got comfortable for what might be a long wait.

Nicole took a minute to think of where she was not too long ago and how she got to be where she is now, working in counterintelligence for Colonel Mathis. Her odyssey began when Darrin Rucker, her partner for more than six years, was killed. They had been pursuing Albert Stanze and Frank McWilliams, who robbed a drug dealer, stabbed him twenty-six times, then strapped an explosive to the body, loaded it into a truck, and tried to blow up the body and the vehicle. Stanze was sentenced to serve twenty-six years to life for murder and robbery at Folsom Prison, but he escaped. They caught up with him and his wife at a Motel 6 on Lawrenceville Highway in the Atlanta suburb of Tucker.

Nicole ran to the building, where she saw Rucker follow Stanze into it. She heard shooting coming from the roof. She raced to the roof, went through the door, stepped out, and saw Rucker standing on the edge of the building with his hands raised when Stanze shot him.

"No!" she screamed, watching as Rucker's body fell from the roof.

Stanze turned toward Nicole, raised his weapon, and fired as he ran for cover behind an air-conditioning unit. Nicole dove and returned fire while lying on the ground.

Stanze kept firing at her as she crawled away before she could make it to her feet and run for cover.

Once she had reloaded her weapon, Nicole stepped out and exchanged fire with Stanze. One of his shots hit her in the stomach as she was firing. Her shot hit him in the chest. When Nicole fired and hit him with another bullet to the chest, Stanze dropped his gun and took several stumbling steps before he fell off the roof. She rushed toward the edge and looked over at Stanze and Rucker's bodies lying beside each other.

While she was taking some time off, Nicole was informed that her lifelong friend, Yvette, her new husband, Pierce Manning, and their family were killed in a car bombing. She was devastated by the news. Before she was permitted to return to active duty, Nicole had to see a psychologist. During that time, she met and fell in love with Jamal Hayes, a programmer with defense contractor Marietta Dynamics. When Jamal received an email that he couldn't open because it was encrypted, the curious programmer wrote a program to decrypt the message. Nicole and Jamal heard this when it was completed and the message was decrypted:

"The man of the future will be of mixed race. That is mainly because so-called mainstream or traditional conservatives are weak and impotent, and they are not advocating for the interests of white people as a group. The Jewish influence, people who hate whites, and the liberal political forces that enable them are the enemy of all tradition, not just the Anglo-Saxon American society it has helped destroy. The niggers and the spics are useful puppets for the Jews in terms of replacing whites. Naturally, they aren't intelligent enough to realize that the Jews are using them, and they will be enslaved once the European race is eliminated.

"The races and classes that we know today will gradually disappear. If nothing is done and unless we, the people, take drastic and immediate action, the Eurasian-Negroid races of the future will look similar in appearance to the ancient Egyptians, and they will replace the diversity of people with a diversity of individuals. That will not happen. We will not be replaced. There are better ways to save the European race from the genocide the enemies of the people have planned for us. We are people who want to preserve traditional Christian values.

"There are four roles that must be played in this revolution: Those who plan the attack, those who spread the truth, those who defend the race, and those who continue the race by bearing children. With the people we have positioned in the military leadership, defense industry, and law enforcement, including high-ranking officers at the FBI, Justice Department, and several members of Congress, we are perfectly positioned to act when the time comes. When that time arrives, and you will know exactly when that is, each of you has your assignment that must be carried out to stave off the genocide that the Zionist forces have planned for us."

Bob Gividen recorded the message. He was a member of a radical white supremacist organization called White America First. Shortly after Nicole listened to the message, a kill team was dispatched.

Nicole heard what sounded like tires screeching to a stop outside of Jamal's house. The next sound she heard was the faint sound of glass cracking. That first shot hit the computer screen.

"Get down!" Nicole yelled, and they both dove for the floor just as a barrage of bullets shattered the windows in his office.

As bullets rained over their heads, Jamal and Nicole crawled out of the office, through the house, and into the garage. They got in the car and started it up. Jamal started to reach for the garage door opener.

"Fuck that. Drive *through* it," Nicole yelled as Jamal floored it and slammed through the garage door. The two men who were standing on his front lawn spraying the house with bullets turned their fire on the car, shattering the back window.

"Keep your head down," Nicole yelled, firing out the back window as Jamal drove away.

When Nicole reached out to her FBI colleagues, she found she and Jamal were charged with espionage and conspiracy against the United States, and they went on the run. That led Nicole and Jamel to conduct their own investigation to prove their innocence. Although they captured Bob Gividen, the pair still faced charges and were arrested. At her preliminary hearing on the charges, Assistant United States Attorney Barnes Watson stood up.

"Your Honor, in light of new information obtained by this office, the government wishes to vacate the charges against Agent Maddox."

"Agent Maddox," the judge said, and Nicole and her lawyers rose to their feet. "You are free to go with the heartfelt apology of the court. This country owes you an apology and our thanks. You probably won't get either, so I'll say it. Thank you, Agent Maddox, and I apologize for ever doubting that you would put your country first."

"Thank you, Your Honor," Nicole said.

Afterward, she was interviewed by Carmen Taylor on her way out of the courtroom.

"Agent Maddox . . . Agent Maddox," she said, but as planned, Nicole kept walking.

"You've been cleared of the charges that were leveled against you," Carmen said as she walked alongside Nicole. "What are you going to do now?"

"I'm going to find the people responsible and see that they get exactly what they deserve," Then she stopped walking and looked directly into the camera. "I'm coming for you," Nicole said, and she and Jamal continued the investigation that nearly cost them their lives on more than one occasion.

When Nicole and Jamal returned home, Nicole saw a man quickly walking away from the house.
"FBI!"
The man turned around quickly and fired at them before he ran. Nicole pulled out her gun and went after him. They exchanged gunfire as he ran to his truck and got in. Nicole stopped and fired several shots at the vehicle as he drove away.

Wondering what he was doing behind the house, Jamal walked back to look. When he saw what appeared to be a bomb with a running timer that showed thirty-two seconds remaining to detonation, Jamal ran back around the house, yelling. "Run!" while waving his arms frantically. "It's a bomb!"

Nicole made it to a safe distance before the bomb exploded, but the force of the blast took Jamal off his feet.

Their investigation uncovered a plot to overthrow the government. However, after that, Nicole resigned from the FBI and eventually went to work for Colonel Mathis and became one of his best operatives.

Nicole had been in Copenhagen, collaborating with the Danish police on a drug smuggling operation. It led to the seizure of 100 kilograms of cocaine during an internationally coordinated operation on a Bahamas-registered cargo vessel while it was sailing south of the town of Gedser, a city in Falster, Denmark. They arrested twenty-seven people.

After her long flight to the States, Nicole checked into her hotel room. After a long hot shower, she ordered room service. When her food was delivered, it also had a card.

The Playhouse, 2:00 a.m. tomorrow.

Nicole took the card and held it over the candle until it burned. At precisely 2:00 a.m., she entered The Playhouse and sat at the bar.

"What are you drinking?" the bartender asked.

"Gin-Gin Mule," Nicole said, and the bartender went to make the combination of a Mojito and a Moscow Mule. When she returned with the drink, Nicole took a sip and looked around the crowded nightclub, wondering why her contact had picked this spot to meet, so she didn't notice when a man sat down next to her.

"What are you drinking?" he asked.

"Not interested," Nicole said without looking in his direction.

"Okay, Nicole, how about this then? You know how to whistle, don't you?"

She glanced at the man. "Travis." She chuckled before giving the appropriate response. "You just put your lips together and blow."

"How are you doing, Nicole?"

"I'm great. You're the last person I expected to see here tonight. Last time I saw you, you were in Juba in the South Sudan."

"And I'll head back there as soon as we're done here."

"What you got for me?"

"Our intelligence says that there is a drug operation that is using the money to fund terrorist organizations in the Middle East and North Africa." He slid her an envelope. "Everything we have is in there. Your assignment is to find them and stop them."

"That's all?" She laughed. "Just find them and stop them."

Travis stood up. "Should be easy-peasy for a skilled operative like you."

"Right."

"Good luck."

"Safe travels," Nicole said and watched as Travis left The Playhouse.

Nicole had been following leads, backtracking the money, and had been told she could find information that would lead her to her objective.

When two men entered the insurance office, Nicole got out of the car and went inside.

"We're closed," one of the two men in the real estate office said when Nicole walked in.

"I'm looking for Godfrey Seagraves. I was told I could find him here."

"Somebody told you wrong." The man stood up and moved his jacket to make sure that she saw his gun.

Nicole chuckled. "I'm getting a little tired of men who think a gun in their hand means they run something. I was told I could find Godfrey Seagraves here, and my sources are rarely wrong." Nicole lied. People had lied to her and misinformed her since she began her investigation.

"Look, lady, I've tried to be nice about this. Now, get the fuck out before I put you out."

Once again, Nicole chuckled. "It's been tried. Let's see if you have better luck."

When both men stood up, and one began to reach for his gun, Nicole reached for hers and began firing. As she moved for cover, several of her shots hit one of the men, and he went down. The other man took cover behind the desk and returned Nicole's fire. She put in a fresh clip. Her adversary took that opportunity to stand and fire. When he did, Nicole fired and hit him with two shots to the chest.

Nicole shook her head. "Why do they always want to do it the hard way?" she asked herself and began searching the office. Not finding anything in the outer office that was of any value to her, Nicole readied her weapon and went into the other office, where she heard a noise coming from behind the desk.

"Come on out of there," she said with her gun raised. When there was no movement, Nicole said, "Let's do this like they do in the movies. I'm gonna count to three, and if you don't come out, I'm going to start shooting, okay? Ready? One, two—"

Suddenly, Godfrey Seagraves bounced up with his hands in the air. "Don't shoot!"

"Godfrey Seagraves, I presume?" Nicole said and stepped forward. She put the barrel of her gun against his forehead. "What can you tell me about a drug dealer who finances terrorist organizations?"

"There's a lawyer. His name is Emil Dudenhoeffer. If anyone would know anything about something like that, it would be him."

"Why him?"

"He represents a lot of drug dealers and people like that."

"Where do I find him?"

"He's got an office on the twenty-third floor of a building at 667 Madison Ave."

The following day, Nicole posed as a client and made an appointment to see one of the attorneys in the office. That would let her know how much security she would be up against. The attorney Nicole met with went to great lengths to assure her that her information would be secure because of their elaborate computerized security system. Nicole left the office and reached out to her contact. She could handle the physical security, but she was going to need a hacker—a good one.

Chapter 21

It was early Saturday morning, and it was Kirk's day off. And this time, he was actually taking advantage of it for a change. Not only did he have plans for the day, but Kirk also planned on starting the day by doing something he never got the chance to do—sleeping late.

That all changed when he got a text message from Beverly Luther, captain of the Major Case Squad.

I need you to check out a crime scene at the Baccarat Hotel on 53rd Street.

"Shit. My fuckin' day off."

Kirk dragged himself out of bed, hit the shower, and headed out. Since Dawkins was working that day, he called her on the way to the hotel.

"What's going on?"

"I don't know. Captain's got me rolling to Manhattan."

"Why?"

"Who knows."

"Well, as much as I'd love in on whatever Cap got you going on, I can't."

"What are you into?"

"Viola Giarratana is out sick, so they paired me with Duenas, and we're on our way to a crime scene."

"I'll let you know what it's all about," Kirk promised, ending the call as he arrived at the hotel.

It was no different than any other crime scene he'd worked. He walked through the lobby, passed the array of uniformed officers, and showed his badge at the elevator.

"Detective Kirkland."

"Fourth floor. They're waiting for you," the officer said.

"Thanks," Kirk replied, and when the elevator came, he got on.

As was the lobby, the fourth-floor hallway was a sea of cops, crime scene technicians, and emergency personnel. When he reached the room, Kirk showed his badge again and identified himself. "Detective Kirkland." He was admitted to the room, and the lead detective, Peterson Hartog, was pointed out to him.

"Detective Hartog." The detective turned around. "I'm Detective—"

"Kirk!" Hartog said with an enthusiasm that took Kirk by surprise. "You probably don't remember me, but you were the lead detective on many crime scenes that I worked. Things were pretty wild back then."

You're right. I don't remember you. He thought of the days he chose to forget. "I'm glad those days are over," Kirk said, wanting to get this over with and get on with his day off. "What you got for me, Detective?"

Hartog knelt next to the body and pulled back the sheet. "Do you recognize this man?"

Kirk took a good look. "Never seen him before. Who is he?"

Hartog stood up. "His passport says his name is Elias Black from Saint Vincent."

"Oh, shit."

"That's what I said when I saw it. And that's when I had them reach out to you. I know you dealt with Black many times back in the day."

"Black does have family in Saint Vincent," Kirk said and put on gloves. He looked at the passport and handed it back to Hartog, who put it in an evidence bag. "Tell me what you got so far."

Hartog stepped back. "Medical examiners already looked at the body. We held it out for you. You wanna have a look before they take him?"

Kirk stepped away from the body. "No need. What you got?" he asked, and men moved in to get the body ready for transport.

"Victim took three shots to the chest and one shot to the head. No sign of forced entry."

"So, he let the killer in," Kirk said, walking out of the room.

"Killers." Hartog turned to a technician. "Let me see those shells. We found two 9 mm and one .380 shell." He showed Kirk the evidence bags containing the shells.

"There were no signs of a struggle in the room," Hartog continued.

"I saw cameras in the hall," Kirk said, and Hartog nodded.

"This is my partner, Detective Nala Hashemi."

"Good to meet you, Detective."

"Same." She showed Kirk her tablet. "This is from the hall cam." Kirk looked at the screen. "They know where the cameras are and are careful not to look at them." She changed to a different view. "Same thing in the lobby. Heads down, moving with purpose."

"Like they just murdered a man," Hartog said.

"Anything else?" Kirk wanted to know.

"That's all we got," Hashemi said.

Kirk nodded. "I guess you guys want me to talk to Black, huh?"

"That's the other reason I had them reach out to you," Hartog said.

"Thought so," Kirk replied and turned to leave. "Mind if I take a picture of the passport?"

Hartog got the evidence bag with the passport and handed it to Kirk. He took a picture and handed it back to Hartog. "Thanks. I'll be in touch."

It was early Saturday morning at the Black residence. Joanne was feeding Mansa, and Shy and Michelle ate the breakfast M had prepared. They were going to visit Barbara in the hospital. The night before, Michelle had told her mother how anxious Barbara was to thank her.

"And I guess you wanna know what happened?"

"Only if you wanna tell me, Mommy," Michelle said excitedly.

Shy smiled. "When I heard that Barbara had met with Jada West and Carmen Taylor, me and Rain went to talk to Jada."

She knew Michelle started to ask her mother why she didn't like Jada, but this wasn't the time.

"One of her men told us where we could find people who could lead us to him," Shy began and proudly walked her daughter step-by-step through how they hunted down Sanders. "When I came out of the house, Rain was running down the street behind him, and I got in the car and went after them. When I caught up, I hit him with the car."

"No, you didn't."

"Oh, yes, I did," she boasted.

"Was he dead?"

"No, so Rain and I shot him," Shy said, waiting to see what Michelle would say.

"Thank you for telling me." Michelle picked up her purse. "This is my gun," she said, reaching into her purse and handing Shy a Sig Sauer P365. Naturally, Shy had seen it when Black bought it for her. Shy stood up, got her purse, and took out her weapons.

"This is my Beretta and my PLR22."

"You always carry these everywhere you go?" Michelle asked because her mother always carried a big purse like that.

Shy smiled. "Mike Black is my husband. I am heavily armed wherever I go." Shy laughed. "That's what I used to tell people when they'd ask me if I was armed. But yeah, the girls are with me if I am out of this house." Shy paused. "We have enemies, Michelle, you know that. So, it's always best to be ready."

"I understand."

"That's why I didn't object too much when your father told me he got it for you," Shy had told her daughter the night before.

After breakfast, Michelle was clearing the table when Chuck came into the dining room.

"Is Mike up yet?"

"No. Why?" Shy asked.

"Kirk is at the gate."

Shy stood up. "I'll go see if Michael wants to talk to him," she said as Michelle returned to the room.

"What's wrong?"

"Kirk's here," Chuck said as Shy left the dining room and went upstairs to their bedroom.

Black was still fast asleep when Shy entered the room and sat on the bed. She shook him gently. "Michael."

"Huh?"

"Kirk is at the gate."

"What does he want?"

"I don't know what he wants." She didn't like Kirk, so she had a bit of an attitude about him being there so early in the morning. "Do you want to talk to him?"

"Let him wait in the media room, and I'll be down," Black said and started to move.

When Black came downstairs, he could hear the ladies in the kitchen laughing about something cute that Mansa was doing. He went into the media room, and Kirk stood up.

"Morning, Detective."

"Sorry to bother you so early."

"That's all right." Black sat down and looked at him. As Kirk sat, Black noted that he'd never seen a look like that on Kirk's face, and he had known him a long time. "What can I do for you?"

Kirk reached into his pocket and took out his phone. "Do you know this man?" he asked, handing Black the phone. He looked at the image.

"That's my brother, Elias. He lives in Saint Vincent. Where'd you get that?" Black handed Kirk the phone and prepared to hear what Kirk had to say next.

"That picture was taken from his passport photo." Kirk paused. "I'm sorry to tell you this, Black, but your brother was found dead this morning at The Baccarat Hotel."

Black said nothing.

A cold chill washed over him that he could feel in his bones. He couldn't believe that Elias was dead. It was the last thing that he was expecting to hear. He and Elias weren't that close. Not growing up together, Black had only seen him twice in his life. But he was his brother, and Black had love for Elias, so he felt the pain of the loss. Elias had saved his life once.

"I need you to come identify the body," he said instead of asking if Black knew what his brother was doing in New York. Besides, it wasn't his case unless Captain Luther put him on it.

Black stood up. "Give me a minute to get Cassandra, and we'll follow you down there."

Kirk stood up. "I'm sorry, Black. I mean that."

"Thank you." Kirk followed Black out of the media room to the living room. "Have a seat," Black said and went into the kitchen.

Kirk sat down, and it wasn't long before he heard crying from the kitchen. Seconds later, Shy and Michelle passed through the living room with tears in their eyes. Neither spoke. As he sat there, Kirk thought about whether he wanted to be assigned to investigate Elias Black's murder. He had long known Black, and Kirk questioned whether he could be objective. Black came out of the kitchen, and that made Kirk think that if it weren't for him, Black would be serving life for killing Shy.

Maybe they would have let him out by now. I mean, since she's alive, Kirk thought.

"Ready?"

"Yes." Kirk got up and started for the door.

"We'll be out in a minute," Black said solemnly.

What was he doing in New York? Black questioned.

When Shy and Michelle were ready, Chuck followed Kirk to the medical examiner's office so Black could identify his brother's body. The medical examiner pulled back the sheet. Black nodded and turned to Kirk.

"When can I take my brother home?"

Chapter 22

Scarlett was happy when Sherraine told her she saw Uncle Mike's car pull into the driveway. Her happiness didn't last long when Black broke the news to her. And then she cried. Every day, Scarlett called her brother, asking when they could take Elias home, but it was five days before the medical examiner released the body.

She cried herself to sleep on the flight to St. Vincent, and her tears flowed again when Scarlett looked out the window as they taxied to a stop. A crowd of family and friends, as well as a band, had gathered to welcome their fallen son home. His mother, Yvonne, insisted that this was not going to be a funeral. It was going to be a celebration of life.

When the Black family got off the jet, they were greeted by his father's wife, Yvonne, his brother, Quentin, and his wife, Kristina, and their daughters, Donna, Janet, and Lisa. Elias's wife Beverly, who was eight months pregnant, was crying and had to be restrained when they took the casket off the jet.

As the band played Soca music in the background, the casket was loaded into the hearse. Once the door closed, the band broke into one of Elias's favorite songs, and the crowd of mourners followed the hearse as it drove slowly out of the airport. It was a parade. Some people followed along dancing, while others walked and sang.

"Where's Daddy?" Scarlett asked her mother as they walked.

"At home." Yvonne looked at Black. "Your father has taken his death badly. He spends a lot of time drinking and staring out at the water."

"I can't even imagine," Black said. He couldn't wrap his brain around losing any of his children.

Once the family had settled into the house, the three children, Black, Quentin, and Scarlett, walked down to the beach where their father sat, staring out at the water. No words were spoken; they just sat quietly with their father. That ended when Fenton turned to Black.

"What was your brother doing in New York?"

"I don't know, sir. I didn't know he was in the city until the police notified me. But I will find out."

Fenton nodded and sipped his drink. "I know you will."

No more words were spoken until the sun began to set in the night sky, and Yvonne called them to dinner. Fenton stood up and faced Black.

"Find who killed your brother."

"I will, sir."

"I know," Fenton said, leading his children into the house to eat.

No one spoke during dinner. Yvonne pointed out that this was supposed to be a celebration, but it did little to change the mood at the table. Elias's empty chair was doing all the talking.

After dinner, Black, Quentin, and Scarlett followed their father back to the beach. Shy and Michelle followed along. This time, Black could no longer remain silent. He had questions for Quentin.

"And he never mentioned going to New York?"

"No, Mike. Not a word."

Black thought for a second or two. "What was Elias into?"

"Elias had invested in weed farms in California and was running a concert promotion company in LA."

"That's as good a place to start," Black said.
"I'm going with you," Quentin said.
"I wouldn't have it any other way."
"I'm coming too," Scarlett announced. Everybody looked at her. "I wanna know who killed him as badly as the rest of you."
"I understand," Quentin said and took his sister's hand.

Michelle wanted so badly to say that she was going to Los Angeles with them, but she had meetings scheduled with the people Barbara was doing business with. Barbara was counting on her, and Michelle had waited all her life for this opportunity. For her, it had already begun. Despite her grief, Michelle was at The Playhouse. With Axe and Press at her side, she played the role of boss of Barbara's crew. It didn't matter that nothing was going on. She was there, ensuring everyone knew that Michelle Black was carrying power, and it was the look of the future.

Elias's body was laid to rest the following afternoon. After the service, the crowd of celebratory mourners and the band paraded behind the hearse to Elias's final resting place. At the conclusion of the inhumation, the celebratory repast began on the spot and ended at the Beachcombers Hotel in the conference and banqueting centre. The celebration of life continued well into the night and was still going on early the following morning. However, at ten o'clock, Scarlett told Black she had changed her mind about going to LA.

"I'd just be in the way of you finding and killing whoever did this to Elias."

"You sure?"

"Yes, Mike. I'm sure." She looked at Shy and smiled. "I'm not a gangster like my friend here." She was a little drunk. Scarlett put her arm around Shy and kissed her on the cheek. "You shoot him once in the head for me, sis."

"I will. You have my word on that," Shy promised, and then she and Black went looking for Quentin.

"Go get some rest. We're leaving at five in the morning," Black said, and the brothers left the celebration of their brother's life.

On the way to the house, Black called Jada.

"Good evening, Mr. Black."

"Hello, Jada. I need a favor."

"Anything I can do to help."

"I need a jet to take my family back to New York."

"Not a problem. When would you like the jet to pick up your family?"

"Reach out to Michelle. She'll let you know."

"It shall be done."

"Thank you, Jada."

"As I said, it's not a problem. And, Mike, once again, I am so sorry for your loss."

"Thank you, Jada," Black said, ending the call.

Jada put down the phone, and a smile crept across her lips. Black had kept her away from Michelle her entire life, and now he wanted Jada to reach out to her. She found that interesting, to say the least.

Chapter 23

At six o'clock the following morning, Jake took off from Argyle International Airport with Black, Shy, and Quentin aboard for the nine-hour flight to Los Angeles. The long flight gave Black and Quentin a chance to talk.

"Tell me about these businesses he has in LA," Black said.

"Elias always wanted to find a way off the island. He'd say the island was too small for him, and he needed a big playground."

"LA."

"He started going back and forth just about every other week about three years ago, I guess."

"What do you know about the weed business he's into?"

"Not much, I'm afraid. I know Elias came home one weekend all excited about it. Somehow, he got involved with a company called Leafy Green, and he would get in the US marijuana market in a big way." Quentin laughed. "He'd show me pictures of him on the trips the group would take to weed farms in different states."

"A group?" Black question. "Are they legit?"

"As far as I know. Like I said, I don't know much about it. You know how we are. We all keep things pretty close to the vest."

"Tell me about it," Shy said and laughed. "Ain't nobody more need-to-know than your brother here."

"We get it from our daddy. If you don't need to know, Daddy ain't telling you shit."

Shy pointed at Black. "That's him. It took me some time to get used to it and—"

"And now you're the same way," Black stated.

Shy laughed. "You're right." She thought about how she had opened up to Michelle and how hard that was for her.

"What about the promotion company?"

"Sorry, Mike, but I know even less about that. All I know is the name, Gage Cast Entertainment, and he's got a partner. Guy's name is Yan Cai. That's all I got."

"It gives us a place to start," Black said.

"I do know where he lives when he's in LA."

"Where?"

"A house on El Escorpion Road in Woodland Hills," Quentin said.

Upon arrival at LAX, Erykah had arranged a limo to take them to the Four Seasons Hotel Los Angeles in Beverly Hills. Since St. Vincent observed Atlantic Standard Time, they arrived just after noon. Once they checked in, they planned to meet in the lobby in an hour. When they were settled into their room, Black and Shy went to the lobby to meet Quentin. When he arrived in the lobby, Black and Shy stood up.

"We need to rent a car," Black said and started to the hotel's concierge desk.

"Aren't you hungry, Michael?" Shy said. "I know I am."

"I could eat," Quentin cosigned.

"I know you're anxious to get started, but—"

"Okay, we can eat first," Black said, and they shared a meal at the fire-lit patio in the Culina Ristorante and Caffè, a stylish, upscale restaurant in the hotel. After they ate, they went off to the offices of Leafy Green.

"Leafy Green is one of the world's largest and most trusted places for cannabis products," the sales rep told them.

"What exactly does your company do?" Shy asked.

"We consult with our clients who are interested in investing in wide-open farms, beautiful ranches on acreage designed for lots."

"Farms? For growing marijuana legally?" Quentin asked.

She smiled. "Yes, sir. The lots are for growing marijuana, legally."

"Wow," he said softly.

"We also consult with our clients on dispensary sales, safe warehouses, large industrial spaces, and the perfect greenhouse for your growing marijuana business. We support your business with buying, selling, and investing. We offer cannabis licensing services, conditional use permits, business planning, and we can even offer consulting on cannabis insurance."

"Are you familiar with a client named Elias Black?"

"Yes." She smiled brightly. "Elias is one of our favorite clients."

"I'm sorry to inform you, but Elias passed away," Shy said. "These are his brothers."

"I am so sorry to hear that. Elias had such a beautiful spirit and that smile . . . We'll miss him," she said.

"Was there anybody you can think of that had a problem with Elias?" Quentin asked.

"No. Everybody loved Elias."

"You wouldn't be able to give us any information about his holdings, would you?" Black asked.

"Unfortunately, I cannot. I am unable to disclose any client information."

Black stood up. "Thank you very much for your time. Our lawyer will be in touch," he said, and Shy and Quentin followed him out of Leafy Green.

"Where to now?" Quentin asked. "You wanna check out the promotion company?"

Shy looked at her watch. "It's after five. Do you think they're still open?"

"I guess we'll find out," Black said, and he drove them to the office where Gage Cast Entertainment was located.

When they arrived, the receptionist was just leaving for the night, but she told them that one of the partners, Yan Cai, was out setting up for a promotion at The Three Club on Vine Street in Los Angeles.

"We're looking for Yan Cai," Shy said when she approached him at the grand showroom.

"And you've found him. How can I help you?"

"My name is Cassandra Black. Elias Black was my brother-in-law."

"Good to meet you."

"It's good to meet you too. These are his brothers, Michael and Quentin."

"If you have a minute, I'd like to ask you some questions."

"What about?"

"About our brother," Quentin began. "He was murdered last week in New York."

"Murdered?" Yan was silent for a second or two. He was finding the news hard to fathom. "What was he doing in New York?"

"We were hoping that you could tell us," Black said.

"I have no idea. The last time I saw Elias, he said he was going home to Saint Vincent for a few days. He didn't say anything about going to New York."

"You haven't heard from your partner in weeks, and that didn't raise a red flag for you?" Shy wanted to know.

"No. Elias came and went pretty much as he pleased. He'd be gone for weeks at a time. Once, it was a month before I heard from him." Yan paused. "He always returned with some amazing story about where he'd been and his latest conquest."

"Was Elias having problems with anybody? Anyone you can think of that might want him dead?"

"No. Everybody loved Elias."

"What type of promoting does your company do?" Shy asked.

"We do reggae and weed festivals in states that have recreational use marijuana. It's been a great arrangement between the two of us. Elias mostly brought in reggae bands from Jamaica, and he provided the products for sale from his farms. I'd handle the concert, the promotion, arrange for accommodations, that type of thing. We've done festivals here in Los Angeles, Colorado, and Arizona, and we were gearing up to do our next one in Oregon."

"Business good?" Quentin asked.

"Booming, with plenty of room for growth."

"Thank you very much for your time. Our lawyer will be in touch," Black said.

"Do you believe him?" Quentin asked once they were outside and heading toward their car.

"No reason not to," Black replied.

"He seemed genuinely surprised," Shy added.

"What do you wanna do now, Mike?" Quentin asked.

"Let's go check out his house."

Chapter 24

Woodland Hills, California, a San Fernando Valley neighborhood bordering Santa Monica, was the next stop for Black, Shy, and Quentin. When they arrived at Elias's house on El Escorpion Road, the sun was just setting.

"This is nice," Shy said as Black parked in front of the house.

"It is really nice," Quentin cosigned. But he knew Elias and knew that he had to live lavishly.

"Is this your first time coming here?" Shy asked.

"Yes."

"This is his first time off the island," Black said.

"Really?" Shy said as they walked toward the house.

"Never had the need."

"You gonna pick the lock, Michael?" Shy asked.

"No need." Quentin reached over the door frame. "Elias is a creature of habit," he said with key in hand. He unlocked the door, and they went inside.

"What are we looking for?" Shy asked as the three wandered around the house.

"Something that will tell us who killed him. At least what he was doing in New York," Black said, and suddenly, there was a loud noise from a shotgun blast.

"Gun!" Black shouted and looked at the massive hole in the wall next to him and then at the woman with the shotgun.

She fired again. "Who the fuck are you?"

Shy ran out the front door as Black and Quentin hit the floor as she fired once more.

"We're Elias's brothers!" Quentin shouted, but he kept his head down.

"Bullshit!" she fired the pump again.

"Good thing she's not a good shot," Black said.

She fired once again and put another hole in the wall over Quentin's head.

"Seriously," he said.

"What the fuck are you doing in my house?" she screamed and fired.

"We're looking for Elias Black. We're his brothers!" Quentin repeated, and she fired again.

By then, Shy had run around the house and entered the back door. She saw the woman firing, readied her Beretta, and came up behind her. Shy put the barrel to the back of her head.

"That's enough of that. Ease off, honey."

The woman froze.

"Now, nice and slow, put the gun down."

She set the pump on the floor.

"I got her!" Shy shouted, and Black and Quentin emerged from cover.

"Hello," Black said.

Shy gave her a little shove. "Have a seat over there."

"Who are you?" Black asked.

"Kashayla Cassidy. Now, who are you people, and what are you doing in *my* house?" she asked defiantly with Shy's gun pointed at her.

"My name is Mike Black. This is my wife, Cassandra, and my brother, Quentin. We really are Elias's brothers."

Kashayla looked closely at the two men. "Y'all do favor Elias."

Black smiled. "It's nice to meet you, Kashayla."

"Nice to meet you." She let out a little laugh. "Sorry about the gun. I didn't know who you were or what you wanted."

"That's all right," Shy said. "I would have done the same thing." *Only I wouldn't have missed.*

"Elias isn't here, and I had to protect—" Kashayla began. "Oh, shit!" She bounced up.

"What?" Shy questioned.

"The baby!"

"Baby?" Quentin said as Kashayla rushed out of the room and went into the bathroom. All three got up and followed behind her. There in the bathtub sat her 13-month-old son. She picked him up.

"This is Elias Black Junior. Sweetie, these are your uncles, and this is your aunt."

"Hi," Shy said and waved. "He looks like his daddy."

Black leaned close to Quentin. "Beverly is *not* going to be happy," he whispered to his brother.

"I'll let Daddy tell her about that."

"Can I hold him?" Shy asked.

Kashayla handed Shy the baby, and they came out of the bathroom. She went into the kitchen and got a bottle from the refrigerator. Then she took the baby back from Shy and began to feed him.

"I guess you know Elias isn't here."

Black and Quentin looked at each other. "I'm sorry to have to tell you this, but Elias is dead," Black said.

"What?" she asked in disbelief.

"He was murdered in New York last week," Black informed her.

Kashayla began to cry hard.

"I'm so sorry," Shy said, putting her arm around Kashayla.

Other than the sound of her crying, silence filled the room as Black gave her time to take in what she'd just heard.

"Do you know what he was doing in New York?" Black asked after a while.

"No," Kashayla said, wiping away her tears.

"Is there anybody else in New York that he might have gone to see?" Black asked.

"I can't think of anybody," Kashayla said, and then she paused to think. "There was a lawyer in New York that represented some other concert promotors."

"Do you know his name?" Shy asked.

"I'm sorry, I don't. Wait a minute." Kashayla handed the baby to Shy. "I may have his card somewhere," she said, standing up and rushing into the bedroom.

Shy held the baby. "Hey, handsome. I'm your aunt, Shy." She looked at Black. "He is so adorable, Michael."

"Don't go getting any ideas," Black said and chuckled.

"You don't have to worry about that. The Cassandra Black baby factory is out of business permanently. We don't need any more children."

"I agree."

"Here it is," Kashayla said, returning to the room and holding up a card. She handed it to Black.

"Edward Drucker." Black put the card inside his pocket, wondering if Wanda knew him. He wanted to find a way to get Wanda off that island *other than Barbara getting shot, that is,* and ease her back into the business.

"When was the last time you saw him?"

"Two weeks ago. Elias said he was going home for a while and he'd be back." She forced a smile through her tears. "We were going to Portland for the festival." Her tears flowed again. "I haven't heard from him since. I know about Beverly, so I'm used to him not calling when he gets down there with her. But when I did try calling him, it went straight to voicemail."

Once again, silence set in until Shy changed the subject. "How did you and Elias meet?"

"We met at a Leafy Green seminar, and I can't speak for him, but it was love at first sight for me. He was so handsome, and that accent . . ." She laughed and wiped away a tear. "I was totally blown that first day. We had so many dreams, plans, things we were going to do."

"I'm so sorry for your loss," Quentin said, thinking about what would happen to her and the baby, his nephew, Elias Junior. Although Beverly would be mad and probably throw one of her famous temper tantrums, he was sure the rest of the family would accept her and the baby as family.

"You said that you had to protect yourself and the baby. Protect from who?"

"Elias was having a problem with a couple of jokers trying to push their way into his business. Said they wanted him to push Yan out. But Elias wasn't interested. He said Yan taught him everything he knows about the promotion business. Elias liked and respected Yan too much to treat him like that."

"You know who these guys are?"

"Not really. We were out having dinner one night, and they were outside. He went out and talked to them. When he returned, he told me about them wanting Yan out, and we needed to be careful because they were dangerous men."

"How long ago was that?"

"A month, maybe longer. He never said anything else about it, but when he left, Elias reminded me that they were out there and I needed to protect myself. You think they're the ones who killed him?"

"I do," Black said.

Kashayla looked at Black. "He told me about you. His big brother Mike, the big-time New York gangster." She looked at Shy and smiled. "And he said you can't be killed."

"That's what they say." Shy giggled it off.

"You find the ones who did this to my man and kill them. And make it as painful as possible."

"That was my intention," Black said firmly.

Chapter 25

"Yes, Pop, you have a new grandson," Black and Shy heard Quentin telling his father. "No, I'm not surprised."

"I feel bad for Beverly," Shy said.

"I do too." Black laughed. "I feel bad for whoever has to tell her. I mean, I've never seen her throw a tantrum, but Scarlett told me it is something you must experience to understand."

"And once you experienced it, you don't wanna do it again." Quentin laughed. "I mean throwing herself on the floor, crying, kicking, and hitting the floor." He shook his head. "Not pretty."

"Like a spoiled little kid." Shy giggled. "Even Mansa doesn't do that."

Black laughed. "He has no need to throw a tantrum safely tucked away in your mother's arms."

"But even when you put him down, he doesn't cry like that," Shy said in defense of her son.

"That's because he knows somebody is coming to get him soon," Black laughed. "Face it, Cassandra, our son is a spoiled lap baby."

"Was Eazy like that?" Quentin asked.

"No. Eazy would just sit there smiling at you like he knew something you didn't. That's why CeeCee's mother started calling him 'Eazy.' She'd say he was easy, like Sunday morning. Now, Michelle, though, was another matter."

"How was she?" Quentin asked.

"She'd cry when somebody she didn't know would try to pick her up."

"When I returned, she tried to do me that way, but I wasn't having it. I said, I am your mother, little girl, and you will let me hold you. But she was much older than Mansa when she used to do that."

Black looked at Quentin. "We're gonna head back to New York in the morning. See if we can't talk to the lawyer Kashayla told us about."

Quentin nodded. "I think I'm gonna stay in LA for a few days. See about his businesses. I may even see if Kashayla wants to come home with me to meet the rest of the family."

"Good idea. I'll talk to Patrick and get him to send a lawyer out here to help you deal with that."

"Thanks, Mike. That will be helpful."

Black and Shy took the limo to the airport in the morning, and Jake flew them back to New York. When they touched down at Westchester County Airport, Michelle was there with Chuck to pick them up.

"Did you find who killed Uncle Elias?" Michelle asked.

"No," Black said. "But I didn't expect to find them out there."

"Because he was killed here," Michelle clarified.

"Right. But I think we know who did it and why."

"We just don't know who they are or how to find them," Shy added.

"There is that. But I wanna hear about you," Black said. "What's it like carrying Barbara's power?"

"It's going good. Things have been quiet at the clubs. I did have to settle a dispute in the gambling room."

"What was up with that?" Shy asked. Despite going along with it, she wasn't in favor of her daughter carrying Barbara's power. Shy thought she was too young and lacked experience, both of which were true.

"Two men were arguing over a woman."

"How you settle it?" Black asked.

"I got them to play one hand of blackjack. The winner gets the woman."

"You're kidding," Shy said. "How did the woman feel about that?"

"Apparently, she had been playing both of them for a while, so she was all for it. Other than that, it's been quiet for the most part."

"That good," a relieved Shy said.

"Well," Michelle said somewhat reluctantly, "I did avoid sanctioning a hit."

"What was that about?" Black asked.

"You know Count?"

"Yeah. He's one of Barbara's runners, right?"

"Right. Well, Count came to me. He thought that one of his runners was skimming and wanted my permission to kill him."

"What did you say?"

"I asked him if he was sure. I told him that my father said always to be right before you act. We are talking about a man's life. Do you *really* want to take that action and then find out you're wrong?"

"What did he say to that?" Shy wanted to know, surprised yet proud of her daughter's wisdom.

"He said I had a point. And I said, come back and see me when you're sure."

Black nodded. His first thought was that she should have called Barbara and let her make the call, but she handled it.

"You did good."

"Thank you, Daddy. And I'm ready for the meetings for her legit business."

"And what are those?" Shy asked.

"She wants to open another club downtown, and she's looking at some properties for condo conversion."

"I'm proud of you, Michelle," Shy said.

"Thank you, Mommy."

When they arrived at the house, M had dinner prepared. After dinner, Black arranged to meet Rain at Purple Rock, and then he called Wanda.

"Hey, Mike. How are you?"

"I'm fine, Wanda. How are you?"

"I'm good. Sitting here with Barbara. They released her today, so we're at Bobby and Pam's house."

"What are you doing tomorrow?"

"I don't have any plans. What you got?"

"Do you know an entertainment lawyer named Edward Drucker?"

"Sure, I know Ed."

"Can you make an appointment for us to talk to him tomorrow?"

"When you say 'us,' who are you referring to?"

"Us, Wanda—you and I. I want you to come with me."

"Is this about Elias?"

"Yes, it is. I'll tell you about it when I see you."

"Okay. What time works for you?"

"Anytime. I am totally on your schedule."

"I will make the call and let you know the time."

"Thanks, Wanda. I'll talk to you tomorrow." Black ended the call then left the house and went to Purple Rock.

"Did you find who killed your brother?" Rain asked when Black walked into her office.

"No. But I've got some leads to follow. His girlfriend told me he was having problems with a couple of guys trying to take over his business." Black paused. "What's going on with finding Barabara's shooters?"

"We killed a bunch of people who were down with him, but there's no way to know if we got him. Jackie tells me that Marvin and Baby Chris will check on a tip. Some guy named Curtis." Black nodded. "You think the two are connected?"

"I don't know."

"I hate it when you say that."

"Well, I don't. If they are connected, that would mean that Sanders didn't send the men to kill Barbara. There is no way Sanders would even know Elias, much less have him killed."

"Agreed."

"But I'm not ruling it out."

Rain got quiet, and then she looked at Black. Something bothered her, but she didn't know how to approach it. "I heard that Michelle is carrying Barbara's power."

"Yes," Black said proudly.

"Would have been nice if somebody told me. I *am* the boss of this Family, and I have to hear it from Yarrisa. Not cool."

"My bad. I should have told you myself."

"You were dealing with your brother's death. Barbara didn't even tell Jackie what she was planning on doing."

"I'll talk to Barbara about it."

"No. I told Jackie to handle it."

"Even better."

It was after five when Black and Wanda sat down with Edward Drucker. He had known Wanda since their law school days. It had been years since Drucker had heard from her, and he was suspicious about what was behind the meeting. He knew who Mike Black was and that Wanda was his lawyer. He was an entertainment lawyer, so he wondered what they wanted from him. *But it's definitely something,* he thought. *Wanda doesn't do things without a purpose.*

"What can I do for you, Wanda?"

"Do you know Elias Black?"

Drucker smiled. "Yes, I know Elias."

"He's my brother."

"Oh, I didn't know that."

"Can you tell me the nature of your business together?" Wanda asked.

"I wasn't his lawyer, if that's what you're asking."

"I am."

"No, we were friends, and I'd give him advice when he'd call. We met at one of the festivals he put on in California."

"Did he ever mention two guys trying to push him out?"

Drucker nodded. "A couple of Jamaicans was what he told me."

"Did he tell you their names?" Black asked.

"No. Just that they were bad news."

"So, he didn't meet with you when he was in New York?"

"I didn't know that he was in New York." Drucker paused. "You mind telling me what this is all about?"

"Elias was murdered two weeks ago at a hotel in Manhattan."

Drucker looked shocked. "My God. I'm sorry for your loss."

"Thank you. Anything you can tell us about these guys would be appreciated."

"I'm sorry, but that's all he said about them."

"Thank you, Ed. We've taken up more than enough of your time," Wanda said, standing up. Once Black thanked and shook hands with Drucker, they left his office.

When the door closed, Drucker waited a minute or two before he picked up the phone and made a call.

"You've got a problem. Mike Black was just here asking about your goons."

Chapter 26

"Fuck it," RJ said and kicked in the door.

Marvin followed him into the apartment, and they started blasting. It had been like that every night since Barbara got shot. Except for the night he was made a captain, RJ was on the hunt.

Whether it was The Four Kings:

RJ stopped, took aim, and fired twice. One of his shots hit one of their adversaries, and he went down. Marvin stopped, took aim, and waited for his target to come into view. When he did, he fired twice and hit him with both shots. One of the men was able to make it out of the building, but he didn't get far before Baby Chris shot him in the back. Judah stood and shot the last man standing.

Or whether it was just RJ and Marvin:

RJ opened fire and quickly dropped back behind the car. He and Marvin were forced to accept that they were seriously outgunned and quickly dropped back behind the vehicle to avoid being hit by the barrage of flying bullets. RJ readied his gun and crawled to the front of the car.

"I'm gonna try to get behind them. Cover me!"

Marvin stood up quickly and fired. RJ peeked over the hood and then began shooting as he ran. The shooting started again, and Marvin loaded the last clip and saw two men coming toward them. Marvin took a deep breath and prepared to engage their attackers head-on. He rose up from cover and began firing his gun, which was empty.

When he did, RJ, who had worked his way behind them, raised his weapon and fired. With their adversaries now caught in a crossfire, the firefight didn't last much longer.

When Mike Black, the boss of the Family, said, "I want this nigga found, and I want him and anybody that's down with him dead," RJ took those words to heart and had been on a mission ever since. It didn't matter who they were; if RJ heard they were connected to Terrell Sanders in any way, he would go after them.

That night, it was RJ and Marvin, and they were at a club called Boss 31 because they'd been told that Barbara's shooter could be there.

"I'm out," Dashanique told her friends, preparing to leave.

"That's her," RJ said.

"Let's go," Marvin replied, and they followed her out of the club.

As she walked to her car, she realized that men were following her, so she picked up her pace. Then she started to run when they began getting closer. Marvin ran her down, and RJ put his gun to her head.

"Please don't kill me. I'll do whatever you want me to. Just don't kill me!"

RJ pulled back the hammer.

"He's not going to kill you. Just answer my questions, and you'll live through this. Understand?" Marvin asked, and she nodded. "Good. Now give me your driver's license."

Dashanique fumbled around in her purse and handed Marvin her license.

"Dashanique Wells. I'm gonna hang on to this." He put it in his pocket. "If you lie to me, I'll be around to see you, and I *will* kill you *and* your family."

"What do you wanna know?"

"You know Terrell Sanders?" She nodded quickly. "He sent two men to kill his sister. Word is you know who they are."

"It was Curtis and the nigga he hangs out with. I don't know his last name, but I heard Curtis bragging that they killed two women in an office building for Sanders, and they were spending stupid cash."

"Where do I find Curtis?" RJ asked.

When RJ kicked in the door and they rushed in blasting, several men were in the apartment. Since they had no idea what Curtis looked like, everybody had to die. One man jumped up from the couch and rushed to get his gun. Marvin was standing in front of him with the pump.

"Shit—" was all he was able to get out before Marvin pulled the trigger and blasted a hole in his chest.

RJ came through the door firing and hit another man with two shots. He went down, and RJ put two more into his head before moving farther into the house, looking for his prey.

"Curtis!"

Marvin moved deeper into the house and fired at the next man who emerged from one of the rooms and hit him with two shots to his chest. RJ fired until his gun was empty, and then he put in a fresh clip.

"Come on out and face me, Curtis."

RJ saw a man run out of a room. He made a break to get to the door but didn't get far because Marvin stepped up and shot him twice in the back of his head.

That was when RJ saw the man in the back of the house and fired at him. They exchanged a few shots, and then he ran out the back door.

"I got him!" he yelled, and thinking it was Curtis, he went after him.

The last man in the apartment fired at Marvin, but he missed. He returned fire and then took cover behind a chair and shot back. When he turned to shoot, Marvin fired twice, hitting him with both shots. Now that the room was clear, he ran out of the apartment to catch up with RJ, but he was nowhere in sight.

RJ saw his prey hop a few fences, and then he made it to the street, but RJ was right behind him, firing shots as he ran. The man turned and fired a couple of shots over his shoulder, then stopped, turned, and shot at RJ. Every shot missed. The man took off running again.

"I'm tired of running."

RJ assumed a firing position, took aim, and began firing until his gun was empty.

"Money!" RJ yelled as Marvin came running up behind him. He slowed to a trot. "Give me your gun."

Marvin handed RJ his gun. He pointed it at the man's head and fired twice, one to the head and one to his back.

When they approached the man, Marvin bent down and checked his pockets for identification. "It says his name is Roger Allen."

"Then Curtis and whoever did it with him are still out there," RJ said, and they walked away.

"We'll get them."

"I know."

Chapter 27

It had been an eventful couple of days for Michelle. It began the morning that her parents and uncle left for Los Angeles. A few hours later, she was awakened by her cell phone ringing.

"Hello," a groggy Michelle answered.

"Good morning. May I please speak with Michelle Black?"

"This is she speaking."

"Are you available to take a call from Jada West?" Caprice asked.

"Yes, I am," Michelle said, sitting up in bed and trying to shake off the deep sleep she was in.

"Good morning, Michelle. Jada West speaking. It is my honor to speak to you finally."

"It's an honor to speak with you as well."

"It is far overdue. I don't know if you're aware, but I am Mr. Black's business partner here in the Caribbean."

"Believe me when I say that I am well aware of who you are and what you represent to both my father and our Family, Ms. West. He speaks very highly of you and your contribution."

"Splendid. I spoke with him last night, and he asked me to contact you about transportation for your family back to New York."

"Yes. I have several business meetings scheduled soon, so I was hopeful to leave today."

"I have a jet en route. It will be touching down in about an hour. The pilot will contact you so you can make arrangements with him."

"Excellent. Thank you, Ms. West. I appreciate it."

"Anything I can do for my Family. It is both my honor and privilege to perform. It was a pleasure speaking with you."

"It was a pleasure speaking with you, as well. Enjoy the rest of your day, Ms. West."

"Safe travels, Ms. Black."

The first thing on her list when she returned to New York was her meeting with Kayla. Like Barbara, she'd been putting off meeting with her while she dealt with her uncle's murder. But now, it was time to get back to business.

"Since we took on merchandise from the Italian distributor Silvo Balassone that your mother put us on to, we've developed the clothing line called Chriscinda, which Chriscinda Parece designed and Barbara approved. She was one of the top designers in the city. And since then, business at High-End Fashions and the In-Town Experience have increased 60 percent."

"That's extraordinary," Michelle said, and Jolina nodded in agreement.

"The line's success with no advertising has also been good for the knock-off Chriscinda line we're selling on the street. I talked to Barbara about changing the name of the In-Town Experience to High-End Fashions to stay on brand and then opening a third and potentially fourth location."

"Let's go see them," Michelle said, grabbing her purse.

After approving Kayla's plan for expansion, Michelle's next task was to close the deal for the space in the

Financial District, where Barbara wanted to open another nightclub. That night, Michelle looked in her closet, trying to decide what to wear. After an hour of looking and trying on outfit after outfit, she concluded that she had nothing fitting for her first business meeting.

"All you got is girl stuff. Fly-ass girl stuff . . . that you look so cute in," she said, looking in the mirror at the outfit she had on. "But that is not the move. Not for something like this."

Therefore, she, Sharkiesha, and Tierra went shopping at Saks Fifth Avenue. After an hour of looking and trying on outfit after outfit, Michelle selected two business suits to wear to her scheduled meetings and two others just to have because these wouldn't be her last business meetings.

"How do I look?" Michelle asked.

"You look amazing," Sharkiesha answered.

"That is you, girl," Tierra said.

"Looking all professional and shit. When are you gonna put us down with the business?"

"Soon, ladies, and it's all happening now," Michelle promised her girlfriends.

The following morning, Press drove Michelle and Jolina to the building where Barbara was looking to rent space. It was Michelle's first time going there, and although she tried not to show it, she was both nervous and excited.

"You got this, Ms. Black," Axe said as he held the door for her to enter the building. He had been at her side since she returned from St. Vincent.

"Thank you, Axe."

Michelle was dressed in a Balmain fitted jacket and bootcut pants, with Stuart Weitzman leather pointed-toe pumps. She and Jolina entered the real estate office.

"Good morning, Jolina."

"Hey, Christine. How are you this morning?"

"Ready for the day to be over. Where's Barbara today?"

"Barbara's not feeling well and is taking some time off," Jolina informed her.

"I hope she's going to be all right."

"She will. However, this is Michelle Black. She'll be representing Barbara's interests."

"It's nice to meet you, Ms. Black."

"Good to meet you too."

"You're early, and Denise is in another meeting. But I will let her know you're here."

"Michelle has never been here before, so is it all right if I show her the space while we wait?"

Christine paused. "I'm sure it will be all right. After all, it will be your space soon. I'll have security meet you there to let you in."

"Thank you, Christine," Jolina said, heading toward the elevator bank with Michelle. Once security arrived and allowed them access, Michelle and Jolina entered the space.

"We're gonna call it The Penthouse," Jolina said, and they walked around the space.

"I don't see it," Michelle said after a while.

"Don't see what?"

"The Penthouse. All I see is a big empty space." Michelle looked around. "Do you have the design sketches Chriscinda created for the space?"

"I got them right here," Jolina said, reaching into her Cole Haan leather backpack and pulling out the sketches.

Now, with sketches in hand, Michelle walked the space and could clearly see Barbara's vision for The Penthouse.

"Now I see a nightclub."

"And I saved the best for last. Come on."

Jolina led Michelle to the elevator. They went up to the roof and stepped out.

"It has a rooftop pool. And we've got permission to enclose it."

"I love it," Michelle said as their agent, Denise, joined them on the roof.

"I am super excited to hear you say that." Denise came toward them with her hand out. "Hi, Jolina." She turned to Michelle. "I'm Denise Getz."

"I'm Michelle Black."

"If you ladies will come with me to my office, we can make this thing happen, okay?"

"Lead the way," Jolina said, and they headed for the elevator.

After refreshments were served, they got down to the tedious business of reviewing the contract. Denise was reviewing the section that was negotiated about the amount of time they would receive free rent.

"I have a question," Michelle said.

"Certainly. What's your question?"

"I was reviewing this section of the contract and comparing it to the construction production schedule, which is very tight. I am interested in discussing a six-month extension of the free rent so the business can become profitable before we start paying rent."

With occupancy rates being what they were in New York City after the pandemic, Denise was anxious to make the deal work. "I think we can work that out. No problem."

"Excellent. Then it's not an issue at all."

"No, it is most certainly not. We want to see you succeed as much as you do. So, I'll move on unless you have more questions about that section."

After reviewing the rest of the contract, Michelle signed the lease, and Denise stood up with her hand out.

"Congratulations."

"Thank you, Denise."

When Michelle got home that night, her parents were there, and she told them about her triumphant day. Once they told her how proud they were of her, Michelle went to prepare for the next meeting. When she called Barbara to tell her what she had done, Pam told her that Barbara was sleeping.

"Don't wake her, Aunt Pam. I'll be out there to talk to her tomorrow after I meet with the property manager."

While preparing for the meeting, Michelle saw something that caught her attention, and her mind began to wander. Soon, a plan formed in her mind.

Press drove them to the real estate offices of Kline and Liberman the following morning to meet with Gianna Ryan. Once they had gone over all of the contracts and they were ready to sign, once again, Michelle had a question.

"Before we get to that, I have a question about another property."

"Ask away."

"I was looking at some of the other properties you have in your portfolio and saw this building." Michelle passed her a printout of the property. "And I noticed that it's been vacant for several years. So, it's basically a tax dog."

Gianna glanced at the printout. "Yes, it has. Unfortunately, the surrounding area had been in decline for some time. There is talk of investment dollars coming in, but at this point, that is all pure speculation."

"I see. I noted that the property is currently valued at $999,995. Would you be interested in an offer of two hundred thousand for the property?"

Gianna sat back in her chair. "I don't know. But give me a minute. I'll run it up the flagpole and see if anybody salutes." She stood up. "I'll be right back."

Michelle smiled. "We'll be right here," she said, watching Gianna leave the room and closing the door behind her.

Jolina looked frantically at Michelle. "What the fuck are you doing?"

"Buying a building. I hope," she said, taking out her phone. First, she called her father and then her mother, but neither answered.

"What you gonna do when Gianna returns and says you got a deal? Where you gonna get the money?"

"I got one more call to make."

"Hello, Michelle."

"Hi, Aunt Wanda. I'm at the real estate office, closing the deal for Barbara, and I just made an offer on another property. The property is currently valued at $999,995, and I offered them two hundred thousand for it. I just emailed you the executive summary."

"Hold on, let me get to my computer," Wanda said. She went to her home office, thinking about a similar call she got from Barbara.

"I tried to call Mommy and Daddy, but neither answered."

"I have it." Wanda took a minute to look over the summary. "I'm familiar with this area and understand why it's been vacant for years."

"I am too, and what the area needs is investment in development. It needs a Fast Cash, Fat Larry's, and other restaurants. It needs dry cleaners, barber and beauty shops, a Laundromat, and a grocery store. It needs insurance agents, accountants, and lawyers—all things Prestige can provide. Uncle Perry can open a satellite clinic. We can even open a community outreach center where people can find information on Obamacare and get registered to vote." Michelle paused. "And there is also a criminal element in the area that needs organizing."

"And you think you're the one to do that?"

"No, Aunt Wanda. I *know* I am."

"You've given this a lot of thought, haven't you?"

"I have."

"Whose name will the property be in?"

"Mine. Will the bank support me?"

"Yes, Michelle. As long as your father *and* your mother approve, the bank will support you."

"Thank you, Aunt Wanda," Michelle said and gave Jolina a thumbs-up.

"Now, listen. You made them a lowball offer, so they will say they can't do that and will make a counteroffer. Somewhere between seven hundred fifty thousand and five hundred thousand. You're gonna come back fifty thousand from your previous offer."

"So, offer them two hundred fifty thousand?"

"Yes. They'll counter that. But where you want to end up is somewhere in the neighborhood of $350,000, but no more than four. And remember, it's a negotiation, so don't jump on what they counter with. They already know what their rock-bottom price is. You just need to find out what that is."

"I understand, Aunt Wanda."

"Good luck, and let me know how it goes," Wanda said, ending the call seconds before Gianna returned to the room.

"Okay. Thank you for being so patient." Gianna sat down across from Michelle. "Here's what we can do. We can take $650,000."

Michelle leaned close to Jolina. "Just nod like I'm saying something important."

Jolina nodded. "We can't do that," she ad-libbed softly but loud enough for Gianna to her.

"Will you accept two hundred and fifty thousand?"

Gianna shook her head and looked at the papers in front of her. "What about $550,000?"

"I would need to speak with one of my primary investors, but I may be able to do $350,000."

Gianna pointed at Michelle. "If you can get your primary investor on board, we can make a deal happen."

"Excellent. Let's close this deal for Ms. Ray, and then we can talk more about this," Michelle said, feeling good about herself because she was *definitely* doing it.

Chapter 28

"You did it!" Jolina screamed when they left the building and walked toward the car.

Axe opened the door, and they got in. "Honestly, I didn't think they would go for it, but they did."

"Well, congratulations, Michelle."

"Thank you, Jolina." She paused. "Press, can you drive us by the building so I can get another look at it?"

"No problem," Press said, and Michelle handed him the executive summary with the address.

He programmed it into the GPS and headed in that direction. As he drove by the building that would soon belong to her, Michelle looked out the window at the vacant storefronts and boarded-up storefronts, speaking of her vision for the area.

"That can be a Fat Larry's, and there's the dry cleaners and the Laundromat," she pointed. "That space looks big enough for a grocery store." Press kept driving. "There's space there for Fast Cash and a barber and beauty shop." Michelle laughed. "And there's the bodega with drug dealers working the spot. I can see it all."

"All you gotta do is convince Mr. Black and your mom," Jolina commented.

"Well, I got Aunt Wanda on board." Michelle paused. "But I need one more ally. Take us to Barbara's house, please."

"You heard the lady," Axe said to Press.

"Ya, sir, boss," Press said sarcastically, but he programmed Bobby's address into the GPS so he wouldn't miss the turn at Wild Ginger Run and get lost the way he'd heard most people did.

Michelle and Jolina went inside when they arrived at the Rays' home.

"Hey, Aunt Pam."

"Hello, Michelle. How are you, Jolina?"

"I'm fine, Mrs. Ray. How are you?"

"Just glad to have Barbara home and getting better." Pam turned to Michelle. "She's in the basement with her father. You can go on down."

"Thank you, Aunt Pam," Michelle said, heading for the basement, thinking her being with her uncle Bobby was perfect since it was him that she needed on her side.

Bobby stood up when he saw Michelle. "There's my favorite niece."

"I'm your *only* niece." Michelle hugged him. "Hey, Uncle Bobby."

"Hey, Barbie," Jolina said and sat down on the couch beside her. Michelle chose not to sit just yet.

"I want to let you know how things went, Barbara," Michelle said, telling her that she had closed both deals and negotiated six more months of free rent to the proposed nightclub.

"That's excellent, Michelle. I knew you could handle it," Barbara said, and then Michelle told them about the building she'd made an offer on and her vision for the area.

"That would make money for both sides of the house," Bobby said, looking at his niece. "You planning on starting your own crew?"

"No, Uncle Bobby. I work for Barbara. Jackie Washington is my captain."

"That's good to know. What does your father think about all this?"

"I haven't told him yet, but Aunt Wanda and the bank are on board."

"Smart," Bobby said, and Barbara nodded in agreement, remembering that she went to Aunt Wanda when she wanted to buy her first property. "You've got my support." He looked at Barbara. "You taught her well."

"I can't take any of the credit, Daddy. I'm sure she learned what she knows from Uncle Mike and Aunt Shy."

"Listen, baby girl, let a proud father take some credit. Like she said, she works for you."

"I have learned a lot from you, Barbara. And none of this would be happening if it wasn't for the confidence you showed in me." Michelle bowed slightly. "Thank you, Barbara."

"Thank you, Michelle, for doing what you did. I wasn't even thinking about the construction schedule and the possibility of time and cost overruns."

"You done good for your family today, Michelle. And you have my total support."

"Thank you, Bobby."

"All you gotta do now is convince your father *and* your mother," Bobby said.

When Roland passed Axe and Press through the gate, Press drove to the house, and Axe walked Michelle to the door.

"Good night, Ms. Black. What time you want us tomorrow?"

"I'll call you in the morning. But you go ahead and handle that business you were telling me about with extreme prejudice."

Axe smiled. "Thank you, Ms. Black."

"And call me Michelle," she said and entered the house.

She saw the light coming from the media room and walked quickly to get there. She tapped on the door, then walked into the room. "Hey, Mommy, hey, Daddy."

"How'd it go today?" Shy asked.

"Everything went great, Mommy. I closed the deal for Barbara's property and made an offer on a property I wanted to buy."

"You did *what?*" Shy asked quickly.

"I made an offer on a property that I want to buy," she repeated. She told her parents how she found the building, made a lowball offer, and then called Wanda.

"And what did Wanda say?" Shy asked, and Black sat there, beaming over how proud he was of his daughter.

"Aunt Wanda told me how to negotiate the deal and offered the bank's support." Michelle paused. "As long as the two of you approve, of course."

"Tell me about this property," Black said, and Michelle handed him the executive summary of the property and told him about it.

Once he and Shy finished the summary, Shy said, "That area is pretty run-down. Are you sure that's the property you want to invest in?"

"Yes, Mommy," she replied, sharing her vision for revitalizing the area. "All things that Prestige can provide. And there's a criminal element in the area that desperately needs to be organized."

"You aren't thinking about starting your own crew, are you?" Black asked.

"No, Daddy. Like I told Uncle Bobby, I work for Barbara. Jackie Washington is my captain."

Black nodded his satisfaction.

"I don't know about this, Michelle."

"Why, Mommy?"
"For one, you're 19."
"You were in college selling drugs at 19, Cassandra." Michael chuckled. "And we're not even gonna talk about what me, Bobby, and Wanda were doing at 19."
"Still, I don't know about this, Michael."
"That's not fair, Mommy."
"Whoever said mothers had to be fair?"
"I can do this. I *am* doing this. I am running both sides of Barbara's business, and I handle it. Everybody but you thinks so."
"Who's everybody?" Shy wanted to know.
"Barbara, Aunt Wanda, and Uncle Bobby."
"You talked to Bobby about this?" Black asked.
"He was there when I told Barbara," Michelle said, and her father nodded.
"How's the other side of the house going?" Black asked.
"Fine. I gave Axe permission to deal with a pressing matter he came to me about with extreme prejudice."
Shy dropped her head into the palms of her hands. "Now she's sanctioning hits."
"I was doing much worse at her age, Cassandra."
"That was you, Michael. This is different. She's our *daughter*."
"That is so fucked up, Mommy. You raised me to be a strong, thinking Black woman like you. My cool Mommy, the businesswoman. But when Barbara got shot, you were out in the street being the gangster you are."
"She's got you there, Cassandra. You *are* a gangster."
"I take it you approve of all this?"
"I do. And I am so proud of you, Michelle."
"Thank you, Daddy." Michelle looked at Shy.
"Okay, Michelle. And it's not that I'm not proud of you and what you're doing. I *am* proud of you. You're amazing. But I'm your mother, and I want to protect you and want the best for you. But your father's right."

"He always is."

"You are on a much better path than we were at 19."

"Seriously," Black said and thought about his body count at that age.

"Okay, Michelle. You have my blessing. Go ahead and make this happen."

"Thank you, Mommy."

Chapter 29

Shy didn't go to work that following day, but she was up early anyway. She called Pooja and Elise and told them she would be available by phone if needed. They both assured her that they wouldn't.

Once she was dressed in a Brunello Cucinelli jumpsuit, Shy went and knocked on Michelle's door.

"Come in."

When Shy entered the room, she found her daughter in front of the mirror, dressed in a Chiara Boni midi dress, putting the finishing touches on her makeup.

"You look nice."

"Thank you. So do you."

"I was going to ask if you wanted to go shopping with me, but I guess not," Shy said, slightly disappointed.

"I'd love to, but I need to stop by the office. Then, I'll meet with Gianna to review the contract and see the property. I was going to ask if you wanted to come with me."

Shy smiled. "I've got the fundraiser for Elaine this afternoon, and I wanted to get something to wear."

"Is that today? I wanted to go, but—"

"What you're doing is more important. Elaine will have plenty more events you can go to. Take care of your business. But I will get you an outfit in accordance with your new style."

"Thank you, Mommy."

So Shy went shopping by herself, with Chuck at her side, of course. She visited a few of her favorite boutiques and got a couple of dresses for herself and two for Michelle before she went home to get ready for the event.

The fundraiser was being held at 583 Park Avenue, a restored church on Manhattan's Upper East Side. When Shy arrived, she was told where the campaign staff was assembled. While Chuck found a spot to watch her, Shy went backstage. The first person she saw was Susan Beason. They made eye contact.

Bitch, I should shoot you now.

"Cassandra," Elaine said, coming out of a room just offstage. "Glad you could make it."

"Thank you for involving me."

"Come on. The rest of the planning committee is meeting in here."

Shy followed Elaine into the room, tried to push away what she wanted to do to Susan, and closed the door behind her. But it wasn't easy. She had her gun and a clear shot.

I should've shot her ass and been done with it.

"I believe you know everybody," Elaine said.

Her planning committee consisted of members of the Association of Black Businesses, Dr. Arlean Willingham, attorney Suzette Joesph, and Felicia Carr. She was the vice president of operations at the Consolidated Life Insurance Company.

"Yes, I do," Shy said.

"So, are you ready for this, Elaine?" Suzette asked.

"I think so."

"Woman," Felicia laughed, "you need to be *sure* you're ready. Don't be going out there half-stepping."

"You're right. Damn right, I'm *ready*," Elaine roared.

"That's what I'm talking about," Arlean said.

"Well, if that's the case," Shy began, and all eyes turned to her, "I think a bit of an attitude adjustment is required on your part, Elaine."

"Me?" Elaine pointed to herself.

"Yes, Elaine, you. You told me you were running to bring attention to issues important to women, people of color, and the disadvantaged. But you didn't expect to win," Shy said.

"That's right," Elaine said, and the committee nodded because each had received the same pitch to come on board with the campaign.

"But if you're gonna do it, you gotta be in it to *win* it," Shy said.

"She's right," Suzette said. "And it is the perfect segue to what I have to say."

"What's that?" Elaine asked.

"If we really are in this thing to win it, I think we need to bring in some help."

"What kind of help are you talking about? More campaign staff?"

"We can always use more volunteers, but I'm talking about somebody who knows what they're doing. I mean, look at us: a doctor, a lawyer, and a couple of businesswomen. Do any of you ladies know anything about running a political campaign? I know I don't. What about you, Arlean?"

"Not a clue. What about you, Cassandra?"

"Not a thing."

"Okay, I see your point," Elaine said. "Does anybody know a campaign manager?"

"I'm sure we could reach out to Martin to refer somebody," Felicia said, referring to Senator Martin Marshall.

"I'm sure he could," Elaine agreed and smiled. "That settles that," she said as there was a knock at the door.

"They're ready for you on stage, Ms. Cargil."

"Okay, let's go do it," Elaine said before taking her seat on stage. She was introduced to a standing ovation. She raised her hands to quiet the crowd.

"Good evening, ladies and gentlemen. Thank you very much for coming out today. My name is Elaine Cargil. I am a mother of four wonderful children, the president of the Association of Black Businesses, and a candidate for the open senate seat in the great state of New York. And I've just been informed that I'm in it to *win* it."

The crowd rose to their feet and gave Elaine another standing ovation. Once again, she raised her hands to quiet the crowd.

"People think that they can't make a difference. We've cried out for justice and gathered in our streets to demand change. We must register, and we must vote. If we fail to exercise our right to vote, we can lose it, a right paid for with the blood of our ancestors. Their sweat, tears, and lives were sacrificed for this sacred right. So, let's stand up for our children, our children's children, and this great democracy. You too can help make a difference."

As Elaine spoke passionately about a woman's right to choose, access to health care, affirmative action, gun control, and police reform and restructuring, Shy was thinking about her children and their future. Not just their future in the Family. She and Black had done everything possible to secure their children's financial future. Listening to Elaine made her think about the world they were inheriting and how what she was doing now with the campaign would help shape that world.

Shy had been thinking about how much time to devote to the campaign and had decided that it would be limited to a few hours with her work schedule. However, listening to Elaine's speech and her own thoughts of the future and her responsibility for it, her mind was changing. Now, she thought that, yes, Pooja and Elise *could* handle things at CAMB and that if they needed her, she would be available by phone. She was all in if they were in it to win it.

"We must unite against the forces of hatred and division and work together for social, economic, and human rights, including guaranteed health care, higher education, better living wages, and labor rights for all the people of this state. We must repair the wounds of racial injustice and build an economy that fights the inequalities of wealth at the expense of those less fortunate. And that, my friends, is why I am running for senate. With your help, commitment, and your vote, we, as New Yorkers, can make it happen. I thank you all for your time today and your attention."

After her speech, the crowd rose and gave Elaine another thunderous standing ovation. And then she and the committee worked the room. Elaine shook hands, kissed babies, listened to the stories of people she had just committed to help, made promises, and raised money. They had set and exceeded their fundraising goal and were very pleased with the event. Once the crowd had left 583 Park Avenue, the planning committee was all that remained. Once Elaine thanked everybody, they left the hall and went their separate ways.

"Wait here, Mrs. Black. I'll get the car," Chuck said.

"No, Chuck. It's not that far, and it's nice out here. We can walk," Shy said.

"You sure?"

"Yes, I'm sure. Let's go," she said, and they started walking the two blocks to the car.

As they approached the vehicle, Chuck noticed a man walking quickly toward them. As he got closer, Chuck watched him reach into his pocket, and he came out with a 9 mm and raised it.

"Gun!" he shouted.

Chuck got in front of Shy, pulled his gun, and fired. He hit the man with a shot to the chest, and he went down hard.

"We gotta go, Mrs. Black," Chuck said, and they started walking quickly toward the car when three more men began shooting at them from across the street.

Chuck returned their fire as he and Shy took cover behind a car. She got her Berretta from her purse and engaged their attackers. When his clip was empty, Chuck reloaded, and the firefight continued. One stood up, and Shy shot him twice in the chest and quickly returned to cover.

"We're not gonna last long here," Shy said as she reloaded her Beretta and the PLR22.

"The Maybach is a block away. I'm gonna make a run for it."

"Okay, I'm ready when you are," Shy said with the Beretta in one hand and the PLR22 in the other. "Just come back for me."

"Ready," Chuck said, and with that, he stood up and began firing as he ran down the street. When their attackers emerged from cover to return fire, Shy stepped out into the street. She started firing with both weapons, forcing their attackers to seek cover.

When Chuck reached the car, he got in, started it up, and pulled into the street. Then he put the car in reverse and stepped on it. Shy kept firing, keeping her adversaries pinned behind a vehicle. Chuck honked the horn to get Shy's attention. She stepped aside as Chuck brought the car to a stop and jumped out, firing.

Shy kept shooting as she moved to the car and got in. Once she was in, Chuck got in and drove away from the scene. Shy turned and looked out the back window. She watched as one of the men with long dreads walked out into the street. He raised his weapon. Although they were well out of firing range, he fired until the clip was empty.

Chapter 30

It was about that same time in the late afternoon, and Black was at Cuisine, the supper club he had opened years ago, when the Family began moving into different types of legitimate businesses. Those days, it was his baby, and Black was involved in every aspect of it. He shaped his vision for the interior, selected the colors, and with Wanda's help, they chose and bought each piece of furniture and the fixtures. He even ran the place himself in the early days.

But that was years ago, and today was sample day at Cuisine, the day the chef prepared new items that he was considering putting on the menu and some other items he just wanted to try. On those days, Black and Bobby would come to Cuisine for a late lunch or early dinner, whichever you prefer to call it. But no matter what you call it, once a month, the chef and his staff would wheel out a table full of sumptuous food for them to sample. As soon as Bobby was seated, they started bringing out the food.

"What's up, Bobby?"

"How are you, Mike?"

"I'm good," Black said.

A server poured each a glass of Rémy Martin Louis XIII, left the bottle, and filled their water glasses. Then they started putting the food on the table.

"We've got one more coming to join us today," he said as the chef approached the table.

"Black, Bobby, how are you gentlemen doing this afternoon?"

"Hungry, Chef," Bobby said. "Pam didn't cook breakfast, so I'm starved and ready to eat. What you got for us?"

"This week, I was feeling kind of Brazilian and musical. As a consequence, some of today's items reflect that mood."

As his staff placed large plates in front of Black and Bobby, he picked up a platter and unveiled his feature item.

"This is filet mignon stroganoff, which I prepared with beef tenderloin, mushrooms, garlic, and cream." He handed the platter to a server, and she placed a piece on Black's plate and then on Bobby's.

"Hmm," Bobby mumbled with his mouth full.

"This is excellent," Black said.

"I'm glad you like it. I will leave you, gentlemen, to have your meal. Enjoy!"

"This is really good," Bobby said, helping himself to herb roasted salmon, sweet potato souffle, and crab cakes.

"It is." Black took a sip of his drink. "That muthafucka can cook his ass off." Black tried the bobó de camarão shrimp, slow braised oxtails, and lobster rolls.

They ate quietly before Bobby said, "What did you think of Michelle's plan?"

"Bob, I gotta tell you, I wasn't prepared for that."

"Neither was I."

"So, I'm sitting there in awe, listening to my 19-year-old little girl unveil her plan for neighborhood redevelopment and organizing the crime in the area, and, I gotta say, Bob, I couldn't be prouder."

"I know. I was impressed, and so was Barbara. It caught her totally off guard. She wasn't expecting any of that from Michelle when she asked her to stand in for her."

"Nobody was."

"Barbara was just expecting her to go to the meeting and sign some papers. But your 19-year-old little girl took over the crew and ran it," Bobby said as Wanda entered the supper club. It was her first time joining them for Sample Day.

"Sorry I'm late." She stopped and looked at the table. "They put out quite a spread for you boys, don't they?"

"They do, so I hope you're hungry. If not, no worries, it won't go to waste," Bobby said as a server placed a big plate in front of Wanda.

"I am hungry. And everything looks so good," she said, filling her plate with salmão, which was salmon, mussels, and tomato vinaigrette.

"You should try the moqueca baiana. It's excellent," Black said of the dish made with halibut, shrimp, mussels, and calamari.

"What does Shy have to say about Michelle's plan?" Bobby asked.

"What y'all talking about?" Wanda said and tried the bobó de camarão shrimp.

"Michelle's plan for neighborhood redevelopment and organizing the crime," Black said.

"Hmm, this is so good," Wanda mumbled with her mouth full.

"Ain't it?" Bobby cosigned.

"What did Shy say?" Wanda wanted to know too.

"She was dead set against it at first. But Michelle talked her down and convinced her she could handle it."

"She is handling it, Mike," Bobby said.

"I know. She gave the go-ahead for Axe to do a job."

There was silence at the table.

"Wow," Wanda remarked.

"Oh, but no. The little boss of the Family didn't just order her first hit?" Bobby said.

"Yes, she did. I expected her to check in with Barbara for things like that."

"So did Barbara."

"Apparently, nobody told Michelle," Wanda said. "But what's important is what you think, Daddy."

"I told her she has my full support."

"So, we're doing it?" Wanda asked.

"She's with the agent, walking the property today," Black said and got some grilled parmesan salmon.

"Good. I'll set the process in motion," Wanda said. "Have they found who shot Barbara yet?"

"No," Bobby said. "RJ's on it, though." He looked at Black. "Mike told them to kill everyone down with Sanders, so you know what that means?"

"The Four Kings are dropping bodies like it's raining," Wanda stated.

"RJ says they got a name now, and they're gonna focus on finding him," Bobby said.

"What about Elias? What did you find out about who killed him?"

"Nothing since I saw you." Black paused while he chewed. "Did I tell you that he has a son?"

"Beverly had the baby?" Bobby asked and got some moqueca baiana.

"No. Beverly didn't have her baby, at least not yet."

"Oh," was all Wanda could manage.

"The baby's mother's name is Kashayla. She's very nice." He laughed. "She's a lousy shot, but she's nice."

"Explain," was all Wanda could manage. This time, because her mouth was full of braised oxtails.

"We didn't know anything about her, so when we got there, we let ourselves in, and she started blasting until Shy put a gun to the back of her head."

"Welcome to the Family," Bobby said.

"You heard anything from Angelo about sitting down with the Montanaris?"

"No, I haven't."

"Is that good for us or bad for us?" Bobby asked.

"I think it's good for us," Wanda said. "It means that this isn't pressing for them."

"I agree."

"So what are you gonna do now, Mike?" Wanda asked.

"I don't know, Wanda. What are *you* gonna do?"

"Do about what?"

"I mean, are you planning on staying up here awhile or returning to the island?"

"I don't know. I kinda wanna do something because, yes, I am tired of sitting around down there drinking apple martinis all day. I'm not ready to practice law or run a bank, but I wanna do something."

"What?" Bobby asked and got some more filet mignon stroganoff because it was so good.

"I'm open to suggestions."

"Well, you could start by hanging out with us. I'm sure you'll find something to get into," Black said.

"You guys are all right, so I guess I could do that."

Once the three old friends had finished eating all they could and talked about everything important to the Family's business, they left a big tip for the staff and left Cuisine.

As Black, Bobby, and Wanda walked toward their cars, Bobby noticed a man walking quickly toward them. As he got closer, he watched him reach into his pocket, and he came out with a 9 mm and raised it.

"Gun!" Bobby shouted as the shooter began firing.

Black dove in front of Wanda and took her to the ground. Bobby pulled out his gun and returned fire as four more men, two with semiautomatic weapons, began shooting at them from across the street. Bobby kept firing as Black and Wanda crawled behind a car for cover.

"You all right?" Black asked Wanda as he took out his guns.

"I'm okay," Wanda said as Bobby joined them behind the vehicle.

Black leaned over the hood of the car and opened fire with both of his forty-fives and shot one in the head.

"Give me a gun, Bobby!" Wanda shouted, and he slid her a weapon.

Wanda joined the firefight as the three remaining gunmen sprayed the area with bullets. As the gunmen fired, Black kept firing. Bobby stood, fired, dove for the ground, and crawled along the ground to another car parked in the lot. Now that he was in a spot where he had a clear shot at the ambushers, he began firing.

With Bobby in that position, Black fired and took out one of the gunmen with the semiautomatic. Wanda rose, aimed her weapon, and opened fire, hitting another of the gunmen with several shots to the chest. He went down but was wearing a vest, so he began crawling along the ground to reach cover.

With the big guns down, Black stood up quickly and opened fire on the remaining gunmen. Wanda and Bobby kept firing, and when one stopped firing to reload, Black stood up and hit him with two shots to the chest. The gunman went down, and Bobby took aim and shot another assailant.

As the last of the shooters fired wildly at them, a man with long dreads came out from the doorway where he was watching the action and ran. He had an AK-47 and sprayed the area with bullets as he ran.

Bobby tossed Wanda his keys. "Get the car, Wanda!" he shouted as he and Black kept firing.

Wanda stood up, fired a couple of shots at the fleeing man as he ran, and then she went for the car. She saw the man she shot, still crawling, and Wanda hit him in the head as she passed.

The last of the shooters tried to run, but Black shot him in the back of his head as he and Bobby raced after the man. He stopped at a bright yellow Corvette, turned, and fired at Black and Bobby. They dove for the ground as the man kept firing until the AK was empty. He tossed it into the car, got in, and dove off. Black and Bobby got to their feet and fired at the Corvette.

Wanda pulled up alongside them in Bobby's Cadillac. She opened the door so Bobby could get in, then slid over to let him drive. Black got in the back seat, and they went after the Corvette.

"Don't you lose him, Bob!" Black shouted as the Corvette got farther ahead of them.

"Sorry, Mike. I can't out-horsepower him in this car. He's got too much vehicle for me."

"Do you see him?" Wanda asked.

"No," Bobby said.

"It's a fuckin' yellow Vette! How could you lose him?" Black asked.

"I don't see him either," Wanda said.

"We lost him, Mike."

"Damn it."

Chapter 31

As they got farther and farther away from the yellow Corvette, Black took out his phone.

"Cuisine, this is Lexi."

"There are dead bodies in your parking lot."

"Are you all right?"

"We're fine. Call Edwina and get it cleaned up before you open."

"I'll take care of it. Do I know anything about it?"

"No. We're shocked that all that went on outside your doors."

"Thanks for the heads-up," Lexi said and got to her task.

When Black ended the call, his phone rang. He answered. "Hello, Cassandra."

"Somebody just tried to kill me," Shy said as she and Chuck were driving away from their shoot-out.

"That's funny. Somebody just tried to kill us."

"Who's 'us'?"

"Me, Bobby, and Wanda."

"Everybody all right?"

"We're fine. But one got away. He had long dreads."

"That's interesting," Shy said. "One of the men that attacked us had long dreads too."

"Where are you?"

"On our way to the house."

"Have Chuck pick me up at Wanda's house."

"We're on our way," Shy said, ending the call and conveying the instructions to Chuck.

"I take it we're going to Wanda's house," Bobby said.

"Yeah, and you stay with her until you can get some people out there. Some guy with dreads just tried to kill Cassandra."

"And at the same time," Wanda smiled. "What a coincidence."

"No such thing," Bobby said.

"No, there isn't," Black affirmed. "So, I'm gonna assume that these are the two Jamaicans trying to push Elias out that Drucker told us about."

"Did he tell you their names?" Bobby asked.

"No. He just said that they were bad news," Wanda answered.

"Yeah, I think ambushing both you and Shy simultaneously makes them bad news."

Black glanced at his watch. "I think I know somebody who could tell me who these guys are, but it's too early for me to call them." He took out his phone and made another call.

"This Rain."

"Meet me at the house."

"On my way."

When Bobby arrived at Wanda's house, Shy and Chuck were already there. Once they saw that Wanda was safe in her house, Black got in the Mercedes-Maybach, and Chuck drove them home. When they reached the house, Rain was already there. She was sitting at the table eating the lemon garlic shrimp pasta that M was making for dinner while she talked to Michelle about her plan.

"Hi, Mommy, hi, Daddy."

"When you finish eating, join us in the media room, Rain," Black said and kept walking in that direction.

"How'd it go at the property, Michelle?" Shy asked, strolling slowly toward the media room.

"It went fine, Mommy. The building isn't in as bad a shape as I thought it would be. But all the same, I made an appointment for a structural engineer to look at the property." Shy stopped to listen. "I made the purchase contingent on a favorable report."

"Good idea," Shy said and continued to the media room, but she was quite impressed.

"Must be something serious," Michelle said.

"I knew that when your father called me," Rain said, finishing her shrimp pasta and getting up from the table. "Let's see how serious." Rain went to the media room, and Michelle was right there with her. She no longer felt the need to wait to be invited.

"What's up?" Rain asked as she walked into the room.

"Somebody tried to kill us," Shy said and told Rain and Michelle about the attempt on her life.

"And at the same time, somebody tried to kill me, Bobby, and Wanda," Black said.

"Any idea on who did it?" Rain asked.

"I don't know their names, but a lawyer who knew Elias told us that two Jamaicans tried to push Elias out."

"And both of them had dreadlocks?" Rain questioned.

"Yes," Shy said.

"I'll put the word out to the captains to have their people start asking questions about these guys," Rain stated, and Michelle nodded. She was in the room, not listening at the door, so she kept quiet, knowing she would spread the word to Barbara's crew.

"Do you think we need to send the family to Freeport?" Shy asked.

"I'm not going," Michelle said quickly.

"*Excuse* me?" her mother asked quickly.

"I said if you send the family to Freeport, I'm not going. I have too much going on to be out of the country for who knows how long."

Shy looked at her daughter and started to say, "you will go where I tell you," but her daughter wasn't a little girl anymore. Michelle was a young woman with responsibilities she'd committed to.

"You're right."

"I don't think we're at that point." Black glanced at his watch again. "I know someone who might be able to tell me who these guys are." He stood up and walked toward the door of the media room.

"Where are you going, Michael?" Shy asked.

"To the office. I'll be right back."

He left the media room and went upstairs to his office. He closed the door and sat down at the desk. Then he opened the desk drawer, took out one of the burner phones, and made a call.

"FBI, Special Agent McCullough."

"Good evening, FBI Special Agent McCullough. Do you know who this is?"

"I do."

"We need to talk. There's something I need to ask you."

"How long?"

"About an hour and a half."

"See you there," McCullough said and ended the call.

"Who was that?" asked her new partner, Special Agent Paloma Morales. She had recently joined the organized crime task force from the financial crime division.

"One of my contacts."

"Anyone I need to know about, partner?"

"No, chica. He's just another contact," McCullough said flatly and went back to reviewing the case they were working on. A mobster named Davide Gaetano attempted to bomb the homes of a federal judge and an attorney.

An hour and a half later, McCullough shut off her computer. "I'm going to call it a day." She stood up.

"You wanna get a drink?" Agent Morales asked and leaned back in her chair.

"Not tonight. I'll get with you tomorrow, though," McCullough said, walking away. "Good night."

Agent Morales watched McCullough until she was out of the unit. Then she shut off her computer and rushed out to follow her.

Petrarca Cucina e Vino, a casual restaurant and wine bar that served Italian food, was one of McCullough's favorite spots because she was into the spinach tortellini en brodo. It was also where she met Black when he needed to talk. The agent arrived at the restaurant and looked around. Not seeing Black anywhere surprised her because he was always early. She allowed herself to be seated and ordered. Her food had just come out when she looked toward the door.

"Mr. *and* Mrs. Black. That explains why he's late."

They came to the table and sat down. "How's it going, Mac?" Black asked.

"I'm good. How are you doing, Mrs. Black?"

"I'm fine," Shy said.

Shy didn't like and had no place for members of the law enforcement community, and even though the FBI agent was helpful to Black, and she once went out of her way to do something for Shy, that went for McCullough as well.

"What can you tell me about two Jamaican drug dealers who wear long dreadlocks?"

McCullough put down her spoon. "Normally, I would say Jamaican drug dealer with dreads, that could be anybody. But I'm pretty sure you're talking about Nigel Paris and Roston Brathwaite. We call them 'The Dirty Dreads.' Drug dealers out of Jamaica. The reasons aren't clear, but they got run up outta there some years ago and set up shop in Brooklyn. But lately, they've been working as muscle for Sanchez Aguilar. That's how they got on the FBI's radar."

"Who's Sanchez Aguilar?"

"He's the head of the Barichara Cartel."

"You know where to find these guys?"

McCullough took out her tablet, accessed the information, and wrote it down on a napkin for Black.

"Thanks, Mac," Black said and stood up.

"No problem."

"Good to see you," Shy lied as she followed Black out of the restaurant, and McCullough returned to eating her meal.

"That was Mike Black, wasn't it?"

McCullough was startled when she looked up and saw that FBI Special Agent Paloma Morales was standing there.

"What are you doing here, chica?"

"Fuck that. That was Mike Black, and you need to tell me something."

Chapter 32

"I thought we were going to Brooklyn," Shy said when she saw which way Black was driving.

"We are. But I need to pick up some stuff first." Black took out his phone and made a call.

"Good evening, sir."

"What's up, Monika?"

"Nothing much. How are you tonight?"

"I'm good. On my way to you, and I need you to have a few things ready for me."

"What you need?" Monika asked and wrote down what Black wanted. "Got it. Anything else?"

"Yeah, I need to know everything on Nigel Paris, Roston Brathwaite, and Sanchez Aguilar."

"I'll get Carla on that right away."

"See you soon."

After getting what he needed from Monika and getting Carla on overwatch, Black and Shy drove out to Brooklyn to the address Agent McCullough gave them for Nigel Paris and Roston Brathwaite. When they arrived at the house, it was in darkness. Black drove around the block and parked up the street from the house.

"Shame you're not here to check for heat signatures," Black said.

"I could have been there, Mike. All you had to do was ask me," Carla said. "Anyway, alarms and cameras are disabled, and smart locks are open. And as a bonus, I repositioned the camera from the house across the street so I can see any cars approaching."

"You're the best, Carla. I'll keep this line open," Black said, and he glanced at Shy. "You ready?"

"Let's go," she said and got out of the car.

Once Black got the items he'd brought along, they started for the house, staying in the shadows until they reached it. As promised, the door was unlocked, and the alarm was off. Shy turned on the flashlight. Not knowing how much time they would have before Nigel Paris, Roston Brathwaite, or both would show up, Black and Shy got ready to receive them.

"What *is* your plan if they show up together?" Shy asked.

"Kill one and talk to the other."

Once they had set up, Shy sat down on the couch by a lamp. She turned off the flashlight and put a silencer on her gun. Then she crossed her legs, made herself comfortable, and put the gun on her lap. Black sat down beside her, and they waited. An hour later, they heard from Carla.

"I got a yellow Corvette coming."

"Acknowledged, Carla."

"You ready?" Shy asked.

"I'm ready," Black said and stood up. "How many, Carla?"

"He's a single."

"Good. We stick to the plan," he told Shy and took up a position by the door. Black readied his weapon.

"He should be coming through the door in three . . . two . . . one."

When Roston Brathwaite came through the door, Black put the barrel of his gun to his head.

"Move and die. Your choice."

"Shit," Brathwaite muttered and raised his hands.

"Cassandra."

Shy turned on the lights.

"Shit," Brathwaite muttered when he saw that it was Black and Shy.

Black patted him down and took his gun. "Walk." He pushed him in the back, and Brathwaite stumbled forward.

With Black's gun at the back of his head, Brathwaite walked into the living room where Shy was waiting. They had cleared the room and put a drop cloth on the floor underneath the ceiling fan.

"That's far enough," Black said when Brathwaite was under the fan.

Shy got up and came toward them. "Take off your shirt," she ordered.

Black hit him in the back of the head when he didn't do it right away. He removed his shirt, and Black snatched it from his hand.

"Hands out."

Brathwaite held his hands out in front of him, and Shy put plastic cuffs on his wrists and then around his ankles. Once he was secure, she put her gun to his head. Black tore Brathwaite's shirt into strips. He used one to gag him and the others to tie him to the ceiling fan. Now that Brathwaite was on his toes, with his arms above his head tied to the ceiling fan, Shy sat down, and Black entered the kitchen.

"I hope pain is something you enjoy," Shy said, crossing her legs and placing her Beretta on her lap.

When Black came back into the room, he was carrying a knife. He made an extended cut down each of Brathwaite's arms and a small cut on his neck.

"You're gonna tell me why you killed my brother."

Black got in his face.

"But not yet."

Black walked to the fireplace. There was a cricket bat framed and mounted over the fireplace.

"You play cricket?"

Naturally, Brathwaite didn't answer.

"I never understood the game. Do you, Cassandra?"

"Not at all."

Black took the frame from the wall and dropped it on the floor. When the frame shattered, he picked up the bat. A cricket bat blade is flat on the striking surface. It is forty-eight inches long and four and a half inches wide with a ridge on the reverse side in the middle where the ball generally hit. The blade has a long handle like a tennis racket.

Black smiled at Shy.

"No point hurting my hands," he said and began beating Brathwaite in the stomach, ribs, back, chest, and face with the cricket bat.

Brathwaite was bloody and trembling when Black took the gag out of his mouth.

"Why did you kill my brother?"

Brathwaite spat blood from his mouth. "Fuck you."

"Cassandra," Black said, and she shot Brathwaite in the kneecap. He screamed in pain.

"Why did you kill my brother?"

"Fuck you," he said through gritted teeth.

Shy shot him in the other kneecap, and he screamed again.

"Why did you kill my brother?" Black shouted and hit him over and over with the bat.

Brathwaite gritted his teeth, breathing hard, but he said nothing. Black put the gag back in his mouth and began severely beating him. He stopped swinging the bat when Brathwaite's chin dropped to his chest, and it didn't come back up. Black checked for a pulse.

"He's still alive."

Shy stood up. "Yeah, but he's not going to tell us anything."

"He's all yours," Black said, and Shy shot Brathwaite twice in the head.

"Search the place. See if we can find anything that tells us where the other one is or why they killed Elias."

"I think I know an easier way to find out where the other one is," Shy said, taking the phone from the dead man's pocket. "Hold his eyelid open, please, Michael." Once Shy unlocked his phone, she made a call.

"Who is this, and how did you get this number?"

"Hey, Carla, it's Shy. I'm gonna send a text from this number, and I need to find the person who receives it. Can you do that?"

"Give me a minute," Carla said. It took her a minute or two to set it up before she said, "Go ahead and send your text."

"Thanks, Carla."

Shy sent a text message to Nigel Paris:

Where are you?

He responded right away.

I'm at Lucinda's

When Carla found where Lucinda's was, she sent the information to Black and called Shy.

"What you got for me, Carla?"

"This one was easy. Lucinda's is a reggae club in Brooklyn. I sent the directions to Mike's phone."

"Thanks, Carla."

Chapter 33

"Just one thing left to do."

"Might as well get to it and get outta here."

Black went to get the gas can that he brought along. He took the can and doused Brathwaite's body with gasoline. Then Black poured a trail that led from the body to the curtains. Once he drenched them thoroughly, he lit a match and tossed it on the curtains.

"Time to go," Shy said, and they moved quickly toward the door.

The house was engulfed in flames by the time they walked down the street to their car. Once inside, Mr. and Mrs. Black watched as the house burned.

"Never before have I just sat and watched a fire like this," Shy said.

"Something I got into when I used to work with Monika."

Their peace was interrupted by the sounds of firetruck sirens in the distance.

"Time to go," Shy said.

Black started the car, and they drove away from the scene. On the way to Lucinda's, he called Carla.

"Yes, Mike?"

"What can you tell me about Lucinda's?"

"It's an old grocery store turned reggae club."

"Layout?"

"There are two levels, a club on the ground floor, office, and storage on the second level. Four exits. The front door and three exits, one on either side and one in the back of the club. A stairwell on the right-hand side of the building leads to the second level and the roof. I'm monitoring police strength and activity in the area."

"Thank you, Carla."

"Good hunting."

There was a small line at Lucinda's when they arrived, so Black and Shy got in line with the crowd. The club was packed, and the music was pounding hard. The dance floor was crowded, and plenty of men had long dreadlocks. Shy stood there, nodding her head and moving to the beat. She leaned close to Black.

"You know it's been a while since you took me dancing."

"It has been a while," Black acknowledged and looked around at the crowd and thought about the chances of them finding Nigel Paris in that crowd. "Come on. Dance with me."

"We're kinda in the middle of something."

"You never know." He took her hand. "He might be on the dance floor."

So they danced because Mr. and Mrs. Black loved to dance with each other. However, since they were in the middle of something, looking to find and kill Nigel Paris, that is, they started looking around for him as they danced. And then they were caught up in the pounding of the music, dancing with each other. They danced until they were tired and went to the bar for drinks and to cool off. They finished their first round and ordered a second round.

"We should have a look around," Shy suggested.

"Since we're here."

With drinks in hand, they wandered around the club looking for Nigel Paris. They looked carefully at each man they encountered with long dreadlocks, comparing them to the image they got from Carla. After an hour of not finding him, they returned to the bar and ordered another round.

"What now?" Shy asked and sipped her rum.

"You wanna hang around a while and wait until the place thins out?"

"No, Michael. He's here. I can feel it."

"Okay, gangster."

"Let's take another turn around the place," Shy said, draining her glass.

Black picked up his glass and was about to drink when he saw Nigel Paris coming out of the men's room.

"Let me see that picture." Shy handed him her phone. "That's him." Black discreetly pointed to Nigel Paris, who was coming toward the bar.

"That is him. Let's get him," Shy said, taking out her gun and moving in his direction.

As they got closer, Nigel Paris looked in their direction, immediately turned away, and looked again. He made eye contact with Black. Paris quickly pulled his gun and fired two shots at Black and Shy before he ran. He saw two signs marked exit and headed for the closest one.

"He going toward the stairway!" Black yelled to Shy, and they fought their way through the panicked crowd after Paris.

Paris burst through the door, expecting to find an exit, but the door was locked with a chain. "Shit," he shouted and ran up the stairs.

When Black and Shy came through the door, Paris stopped and fired a few shots at them. They pressed their backs against the wall until the shooting stopped. Paris got to the second level and tried the doorknob. It was locked, so he fired a few more shots at Black and Shy and continued up the steps to the roof. He continued firing when he got to the door before he ran out on the roof. Paris ran to an air-conditioning unit and reloaded his gun. He aimed at the door and waited for Black and Shy to come out.

When Black came through the door, Paris began firing. The shots hit the door, and Black and Shy retreated to the stairway. They reloaded their weapons. Black peeked out, and Paris fired several more shots.

"You think you can make it to the AC unit over there?" Black asked and pointed.

Shy peeked out, and Paris fired again.

"I can make it." Shy readied her weapon. Black stood up with a gun in each hand.

"Push the door open and run when I start shooting," he said.

Shy pushed the door open. He began firing with both weapons, and Paris ducked behind the AC unit for cover. Shy came out of the stairway, firing at Paris as she ran to the AC unit. When she arrived, Shy kept firing, pinning Paris down until Black made it out of the stairway. He ran to the AC unit, firing. When he got there, he kept firing while Shy reloaded.

Paris reloaded his weapon and exchanged fire with Black and Shy until his gun was empty. He looked over his shoulder at the building next to them and thought he had no choice. He stood up, ran for the edge, and leaped across the alley toward the next building. When Black and Shy got to the edge of the building, Paris was hanging on to the edge of the building across the alley. He lost his grip and fell the three stories to the ground.

"You think he's dead?" Shy asked as they looked down.

"No, he's moving," Black said, and they hurried down the fire escape to the alley. When they approached Paris, it was easy to see from the bone hanging out that his leg was broken.

"Please, you got to call me an ambulance," Paris said, trying to get up.

"Tell me why you killed my brother, and I'll call you an ambulance."

"Aguilar wanted your brother dead."
"Why?"
"I don't know why. Now call me an ambulance."
"Let's go, Michael," Shy said and turned to walk away.
"Wait."
"Why did Aguilar want my brother killed?"
"I don't know why, but it was about Alamilla Delgado."
"Who is she?" Black demanded to know.
"She Aguilar's woman."
"Where is she?"
"She ran away from Aguilar and is hiding somewhere. I don't know where. Now, please, call me an ambulance."
"About that . . . You killed my brother." Black and Shy took out and pointed their guns at Paris. "You really didn't believe I was gonna let you live, did you?" Black shot Paris twice in the chest. Shy put one in his head.

"Getting kinda fond of those head shots, aren't you?" Black asked as they left the alley and walked to their car.

"One to the head to make sure they're gone was what I was taught."

"Who taught you that?"

"You did."

When they reached the car and had driven away from Lucinda's, Black made another call to Carla. "I promise this is the last time tonight."

"What you got for me?" she asked.

"I need to know everything about Alamilla Delgado."

"Who's she, Mike?"

"She's Sanchez Aguilar's woman. She's in hiding, so I need to know where she is."

"I'm on it, Mike."

"I knew you would be. Good night, Carla. We'll talk tomorrow."

"Good night, and say good night to Shy."

"I will," Black said and ended the call. "Carla said good night."

"All I wanna do is come out of this dress and these heels and relax in a hot tub," Shy said and relaxed in her seat for the ride out to New Rochelle, knowing that even though Nigel Paris and Roston Brathwaite, the so-called Dirty Dreads, were dead, this was far from over.

Chapter 34

The Playhouse. The house that Barbara built. It was just another hole-in-the-wall bar and gambling club called Sweet Nectar before Jackie Washington handed it to Barbara when she got too big for Conversations. Barbara renovated it, expanded the spot, and transformed it into one of the moneymaking jewels of the Family's business.

But that night, while Mr. and Mrs. Black were out hunting in Brooklyn, The Playhouse served as a meeting place for Nicole Maddox. When she told her contact that she needed a hacker, her contact told her to come to The Playhouse and wait at the bar. The hacker would contact her there.

It wasn't her first time coming there for a meeting. When she received her assignment, Nicole met her contact, Travis Burns, at The Playhouse. Colonel Mathis had assigned the former FBI agent to track down and stop a drug dealer who was using his drug profits to fund terrorist organizations in the Middle East and North Africa.

After standing in line to get in, Nicole went to the bar and ordered a drink.

"Gin-Gin Mule?" the bartender asked.

"You remembered."

"I never forget a face or a drink."

While waiting for the bartender to fix her drink, she looked around at The Playhouse crowd and wondered why this seemed a preferred meeting spot for the

Colonel's operatives, or at least the ones she'd dealt with for this mission. She'd been in a few places like The Playhouse during her FBI days, so she knew that there was gambling going on there.

"Gin-Gin Mule courtesy of the gentleman at the end of the bar," the bartender said and placed the drink in front of Nicole. She looked at the man at the end of the bar. He raised his glass, and Nicole took out her money.

"Thank the gentleman, but no, thank you. I pay for my own drinks."

"A wise practice."

As Nicole sipped her drink, she looked around the packed dance floor. It reminded her that she hadn't been dancing in years. Although she was there to meet her contact, she thought that if some good-looking man asked her to dance, she would consider it.

"Naw."

Nicole had been there for an hour and was on her third Gin-Gin Mule, so she wondered if her contact would show.

"Nicole?"

She turned around, and there was Zoey Anderson. Nicole knew her from the days when she was on the run from the FBI when she and her boyfriend, Jamal Hayes, were charged with espionage and conspiracy against the United States. She worked with Jamal at Marietta Dynamics and was instrumental in helping clear them of all charges and uncovering the plot to overthrow the government.

"Zoey?"

"Yes, how are you, Nicole?"

"I'm doing great. What about you?"

"I've been doing great too. It is so good to see you. How's Jamal?"

"He's fine. I talked to him a couple of days ago. He's working for a software developer and living in California in a small town outside of Sacramento, enjoying the quiet life."

"Good for him. I'm glad he landed on his feet."

"He deserved it after what we went through."

"So, you guys aren't together anymore?"

"We are. It's a very long-distance relationship. I travel a lot for work, so I see him when I'm on the West Coast."

"What are you drinking, Zoey?" the bartender asked.

"Negroni."

"Coming up. Another Gin-Gin Mule?" he asked.

"Please," Nicole said, and the bartender went to fix their drinks.

"Is the very long-distance thing working?" Zoey asked.

"It is. After our ordeal, I quit the FBI, and we tried to make a go of it. We were happy. We moved to that small godforsaken town." Nicole laughed and sipped her drink. "I went back to school and passed the bar. I went as far as interviewing for a job with a prestigious law firm in Sacramento."

"Did you get the job?"

"I did. But on the day I was supposed to start work, I got as far as the parking lot before I realized that being a lawyer wasn't what I wanted to do. I'm a cop. It's in the blood. But I didn't want to go back to the FBI, so I called a friend, and he got me into a position I was better suited for."

"How did Jamal take it?"

"He understood. He was expecting it." Nicole laughed as the bartender returned with their drinks. "The entire time I was studying for the bar and hating it, Jamal kept asking me if I was sure that was what I wanted to do. I would tell him that I was, but now, I realize I was just saying that because it was what he wanted for me."

"Not what you wanted for you. I hear that and can relate."

"What about you? I'm guessing you're not with Marietta Dynamics anymore?"

"No, Nicole." Zoey frowned and sipped her drink. "I am not, " she said, and the nightmare she experienced came rushing back to her mind.

"Sounds like your parting with Marietta Dynamics wasn't pretty."

"It wasn't. About a month after you and Jamal left, Marietta Dynamics fired me for hacking their server. Two days later, the police are at my door. . . ."

"Oh, no."

"Oh, yes. The police bring me to the station for questioning. I tell them my story. They say thank you for coming in, and they release me. That next week, the FBI is at my door. They bring me to the station for questioning. I tell them the exact same story that I told the police. They thank me, and I go home." Zoey shot her drink and signaled for another. "Two days later, they're back. Only this time, they arrest me for espionage and conspiracy against the United States."

"I had no idea, Zoey. I am sorry that happened to you."

"Me too. Believe that."

"What happened with that?"

"They eventually dropped the charges and released me," she said without telling Nicole how the charges were eventually dropped.

"Good. Did you tell them that you were working with the FBI?"

"I did. And every time I'd say Agent Maddox, they'd correct me and say *former* Agent Maddox."

"What agent did you have interviewing you?"

"Agent Yastrzemski."

"That racist prick. He always hated me."

"And it showed. It was like he wanted to prove you were really a traitor."

"Well, I'm glad you got outta there, and you seem to have landed on your feet."

"Yeah, I've done all right working jobs that utilize my skill set."

"Good for you."

The bartender placed drinks in front of the ladies.

"Thank you." Zoey sipped her drink. "What brings you to New York?"

"I'm here on business."

Zoey looked around. "And what brings you to The Playhouse?"

"I'm here to meet somebody," Nicole said.

"I'm here to meet somebody too." Zoey looked at the former agent. "Unless . . .?" she questioned and paused before she recited the recognition code. "You better sing one verse for us. What we gotta do?"

"We gotta have a funky good time. Oh, yeah," Nicole said, smiling after responding correctly to the recognition code.

"I guess I'm here to meet you."

"And you must be the hacker I need."

"At your service."

"You work for Colonel Mathis, I take it?"

"Yes. After I decided not to chain myself to a desk, I called Major Cutter, and he put me in touch with the Colonel. I have been working for him ever since. What about you? How did you get hooked up with the Colonel?"

"When I was released from prison and walked outside, there was Major Cutter. He was the only reason that they let me go. It was he who got the FBI to drop the charges. He said he was out of the country and apologized for not getting me out sooner. He told me if I ever needed anything, all I had to do was call. Well, when I tried to get a job—any job—I couldn't. Marietta Dynamics blackballed me in the industry. I couldn't even get an entry-level programmer job. So, I reached out to the Major. Like you, he put me on the Colonel. He got me to move here to New York, and I do occasional jobs for him and others. The work is mostly legal. Some of it isn't. But it keeps a roof over my head, and I eat every day. So, it's all good."

Nicole raised her glass. "To all good."

"I will drink to that."

They drained their glasses, and Nicole signaled for around round.

"Now, you need a hacker, right?"

"I do."

"What's the job? If you can tell me and not have to kill me, that is."

"My mission is to track down a drug dealer who uses the drug proceeds to fund terrorist organizations in the Middle East and North Africa."

"What's his name?"

"That's the thing. Nobody knows his name. So, I've been backtracking. Following the money back to its source."

"What can I do for you?"

"The job for you is twofold. I need you to hack the FBI for information about two Jamaican drug dealers named Nigel Paris and Roston Brathwaite, and I need to break into a lawyer's office. His name is Emil Dudenhoeffer, and the material I need is on an air-gapped computer."

"So, you need me to hack the password."

"Not only that, but there are also several security protocols that will need to be defeated, and they can only be accessed from within the property."

"Got ya. It sounds to me like a two-person job."

"Why two?"

"Because I can't be in two places at the same time. I need to defeat the security protocols for one location and hack the air-gapped computer in another. I could do one and then the other, but I would much rather have someone to monitor what's going on in case anything goes wrong. And besides, having someone on overwatch to let us know if anyone is coming while I'm hacking the computer and downloading files is always a good idea. After my week in prison, I know I never wanna go back. Best to take security precautions on the front rather than be running from cops on the back end."

"I couldn't agree more. And I know what you mean about going back to prison."

Zoey finished her drink. "So, *former* FBI Agent Maddox, let's go hack your former mates."

Nicole finished her drink, paid the tab, tipped the bartender, and then she left The Playhouse and followed Zoey to her house. When they arrived, Zoey wasted no time getting set up, and since she had hacked the FBI before, she had no problem getting in. She easily accessed the information on Nigel Paris and Roston Brathwaite.

"That's interesting," Zoey said once she provided Nicole with the requested information.

"What's that?"

"The last agent to access this file was Agent Bridgette McCullough."

"Mac. So, she's assigned to the organized crime unit here in New York. Good to know. I'll reach out to her if the need arises."

Chapter 35

After leaving Lucinda's and driving home from Brooklyn, Shy could come out of the Balmain midi dress she'd been wearing all day, and the Rene Caovilla slingback pumps that were hurting her feet by that time, and she relaxed in a hot tub.

"I'll be waiting for you when you come out," Black said after a quick shower.

However, when Shy got out of the bathtub, hot, refreshed, and ready, she found her husband fast asleep and snoring. She shook her head, put on her Natori satin and lace slip, and got in bed next to Black. She kissed his back.

"Good night, Michael."

It was almost noon when Black woke up the following day. He looked over, surprised that Shy was still in bed with him. He was sure she'd be going today since she didn't go to the office the day before. But there she was, his beautiful wife, dressed in red satin and lace, still fast asleep.

Not wanting to disturb her while she was sleeping, Black eased out of bed, put on some clothes, and went into his office to make some calls. His first call was to Monika and Carla. They had just begun searching for information about Alamilla Delgado and Sanchez Aguilar.

"I haven't got anything you can use yet. I'll give you a call when I do," Monika said, ending the call and returning to work.

His next call was to Rain. "Come out to the house. Let's talk."

"I'll be there in about an hour," she replied.

After looking in on Shy, Black went downstairs to the kitchen. M and Joanne were in there with Mansa. They had just finished lunch, and Joanne had been cleaning up after Mansa since he had fed himself.

"Afternoon."

"Afternoon, Michael," both of the Golden Girls said.

Black wiped his son's face and picked him up. "What's up, big boy?"

"What can I get you to eat?" M asked.

"What did y'all have?"

"We had BLT turkey salad, but I could make you something else. Cassandra is still home, isn't she?"

"Still asleep."

"Sit, and I'll make something for both of you."

Black sat at the table. "What did you have in mind?"

"I don't know. What do you have a taste for?" she asked and placed the last of the salad in front of him.

"Whatever is easy," he said, and he started eating with Mansa in his arms, thinking he was just as guilty as the women in the house.

"You want me to take him, Michael?" Joanne asked and took him from Black.

"Thank you." He continued eating. "Oh, and Rain is on her way out here."

"You know that child is always hungry," Joanne said. "Better cook enough for her too."

"And you know, since it's Rain, she's gonna go all out," Black said, and when he finished his salad, he took Mansa from Joanne and left the kitchen.

"Let's go jump up and down on the bed and wake up Mommy."

***

Black, Shy, and Mansa were in the media room when William came to let them know that Rain was there, and he showed her in. The first thing she did was pick up Mansa. Rain didn't have any children or want any, but she absolutely loved everybody else's kids.

"How's my man today?"

Shy chuckled. "Don't let Eazy hear you say that. You know he still thinks he's your man."

"Eazy just gonna have to understand I'm in love with this little handsome man."

It was then that M came into the media room. "I didn't know you had gotten here, Rain."

"Hey, Ms. Black," she said, making faces at Mansa.

"Y'all come on, lunch is ready," M said and turned to leave.

Because Rain had come to lunch, instead of cooking something easy, M made some more BLT turkey salad, a stir-fry with broccoli and shrimp, mushroom pasta, green bean slaw, and cheesy garlic bread that she made with Colby Jack and mozzarella cheeses.

"Everything looks and smells delicious, Ms. Black," Rain said and sat at the dining room table. Joanne came and got Mansa, so Rain could eat. At the conclusion of their meal, the three returned to the media room.

"What's up?" Rain asked.

"Nigel Paris and Roston Brathwaite are dead."

"They're the ones that killed your brother, right?"

"Yes."

"They tell you why they killed him?"

"No. But they were working as muscle for Sanchez Aguilar."

"Who's Sanchez Aguilar?"

"He's the head of the Barichara Cartel."

"Never heard of them," Rain said.

"Neither have I," Black stated. "I got Monika and Carla checking on him. But whatever the reason why they killed Elias, it has something to do with a woman named Alamilla Delgado."

"What about her?" Rain asked.

"Knowing your brother, he was probably fuckin' her too," Shy said.

"You're probably right," Black agreed, thinking it ran in the family as he was quite the ladies' man before meeting Shy, who changed his life. "Anyway, she's supposedly somewhere hiding from him. I got Monika and Carla looking into her and Sanchez Aguilar, but I want you to get everybody on this."

"What about Barbara and finding this Curtis guy and whoever was with him?"

"That's important too. RJ needs to stay on that."

"Okay. Now, let's talk about Michelle."

"What about Michelle?" Shy asked defensively.

"How much power does she have?"

"As far as I'm concerned, she's carrying Barbara's power."

"For now. Black, you gotta know that since she's y'all daughter, people naturally assume that her power and authority come from you."

Black nodded and thought about whether that assumption was reasonable for Michelle. "I see your point."

"I need to know."

"You are the boss of this Family. So, in the future, you need to talk about that with her captain."

"I did." Rain paused. "I talked with Jackie, and she's concerned too."

"She has no power other than what you, Jackie, and Barbara allow her. Therefore, when you need to reign her in, reign her in."

"Okay."

"Anything else?" Black asked.

"That's all I got." She paused. "You heard anything from Angelo about sitting down with the Montanaris?"

"Not yet. But we have been into a lot since I talked to him." Black smiled at Rain. "You know you could call Angelo yourself. You *are* the boss of this Family."

"So you and everyone else keep telling me." Rain stood up. "I'm out."

When she was heading for the door to leave, Black's phone rang, and he answered,

"What you got?" he asked, seeing that it was Monika calling.

"It's not much, but it's enough to get you started. Come on in when you're free, and I'll tell you all about it."

"Cassandra and I are on our way to you now."

"Monika?" Shy questioned as she walked alongside Rain.

"Yeah, she's got something."

"I'll go put something on," Shy said as they reached the door.

"What's wrong with what you have on?" Black asked as he opened the door for Rain. She was wearing jeans and an old Baby Got Back sweatshirt. Shy looked at Black like he should know better and said nothing.

"See you, Shy," Rain said as Shy waved and went up the stairs.

When Shy returned to the media room where Black was impatiently waiting, she wore a Camilla baroque jumpsuit. "What are you sitting around for? I'm ready," she said, and Black stood up. "Chuck's already got the car out front, and here you are dragging along."

"*Really,* Cassandra?" Black said and followed her out the door.

Monika and Carla were waiting to give him what little information they had on Alamilla Delgado and Sanchez Aguilar when they arrived at the office. They put her image up on the screen.

"She very pretty, Michael."

"Yeah. Kinda makes me think you were right, and this is about him fuckin' her," Black cosigned.

"Alamilla Delgado," Carla began. "The third child of Isabella and Santiago Delgado. Twenty-seven years old, born in Cartagena, Colombia. Her parents migrated to New York when she was 10. Graduated Monsignor McClancy Memorial High School and attended Nassau Community College but didn't graduate. She has no employment record; she has never paid rent anywhere that I can see. The only bill that has ever been in her name is a cell phone from three years ago. Other than that, your girl is a ghost."

"Sounds like a woman somebody has been taking care of," Shy said.

"It's unclear when or where she met Aguilar, but we're still digging into that," Monika said. "What we can tell you is that she's hiding out somewhere in the Dominican Republic."

Chapter 36

Over the last few days, Zoey had been busy checking out the building and reviewing the security protocols to accomplish the mission: break into a law firm and copy files from an air-gap computer, a security measure that isolated the laptop and prevented it from establishing an external connection. An air-gapped computer is physically segregated and incapable of connecting wirelessly or physically with other computers or network devices.

"Encoded ID cards control the entrance to the building."

"I can take care of that," Nicole said. "I know a guy. And conveniently enough, Lorenzo recently moved his operation to New York."

"Two questions."

"Shoot."

"Does he do good work?"

"Yes. He was the best at it. I arrested him once before."

"Does he know you're not FBI anymore?"

"He does."

"And he'll still help you?"

"For the right price, of course."

"Second question. Can he be trusted? Especially now that you aren't FBI any longer."

"Yes. Even though I'm not FBI now, I can still get a team of agents to show up and tear a place apart."

"Good to know," Zoey laughed. "You know, in case we need the FBI to bail us out."

"It's a good power to have."

"Any who, once we get in the building, we'll need to take control of the cameras. Card readers also allow access to each area of the building. That includes offices, the server room, shit, even the break room is controlled access. The only place you can go without a card is the bathroom. So, your guy needs to be good."

"He is."

"Okay. I've got a third person to handle the cameras. Her name is Garrika Peters."

"Same question for you."

"What, is she good?"

"Yes."

"She's not as good as me, but nobody is. However, she's got the skills needed to get the job done."

"Okay."

"Now, to avoid drawing attention to ourselves, we will need to be in the building at eight o'clock in the morning. If all goes well, we're a go at five thirty."

"So, what do we do all day?"

"You're not going to like it."

"Tell me."

"Your cover is Sheila Bradford. You're a lawyer reporting for your first day at work."

"You're kidding?"

"I'm not."

"Suppose my new supervisor decides to contact HR about his new employee?"

"We'll be set up for Garrika to receive that call. And even if she doesn't get the call for some reason, I've already uploaded all the new hire information to their HR servers." Zoey handed Nicole a piece of paper. "There is your background cover information. Study it and be ready to answer any questions that may come your way."

"Got it."

"I'll be going in as part of the housekeeping staff, so I can float and handle anything that might come up. Garrika will be going in as an actual employee because we'll be accessing the security systems from their office. The employee's name is Megan Manning."

"What about the real Megan Manning?"

"I got that handled. My sometimes partner, Press, will take care of that."

"How, if you don't mind me asking?"

"Sure. She has a drinking problem and likes to frequent The Red Lion on Bleecker Street. It's a bar with live music. Press will slip something in her drink, take her home, and babysit until we're done."

"Sounds like a plan."

"Like I said, we're a go at five thirty. The issue is your new department gets off at five."

"So, do you have a plan for what I will do during that thirty-minute window?"

"Hang out in the law library. Whatever you get to work on during the day, tell them that you're doing some research to establish a precedent."

"That should impress them . . . unless they call my bluff." Nicole giggled.

"I'm sure you're good at thinking on your feet."

"I am."

"Let's go see your guy. I'll have Garrika meet us there."

Once the trio met with Lorenzo, and he took their pictures, Zoey and Garrika left, and Nicole stayed with Lorenzo until he had the encoded IDs ready.

"These will get the job done. I guarantee it," he said as he handed Nicole the cards.

"They better. I still have friends."

"Now, why you gotta go there? I mean, here we are, two people doing business, and you gotta drag in threats of FBI involvement? Not cool, Nicole, not cool at all."

"Sorry. Old habits."

The following day, at seven fifty-five, Zoey and Garrika presented their encoded IDs to the security personnel at the maintenance entrance. At the same time, Nicole, the new employee, appeared at the main entrance and was told to wait. She sent Zoey a text message. When Zoey received the text, she went to the main entrance in time to see another employee greet Nicole, and he escorted her to their work area. The remainder of the day went how the group needed it to, and at precisely five thirty, Zoey sent a text.

We're a go.

Once Garrika sent a text verifying that she had control of the cameras, Nicole left the law library, and Zoey began making her way to the office of Emil Dudenhoeffer. She arrived before Nicole did and sent a text to Garrika, who disabled the lock on the office door, and she entered.

I'm in.

When Nicole arrived, she wasted no time attaching a password-cracking tool to the safe and allowed it to do its work. The tool used several different methods, including dictionary attack, brute force attack, rainbow table attack, and cryptanalysis.

It took half an hour, but when the safe opened, Zoey got the air-gapped computer and went to work using some of the same techniques to access the files that Nicole said she needed.

"I'm in," Zoey said. "Accessing the files in question."

Once she accessed them, she inserted a thumb drive and began her download. Both women watched the percentage of the download completed inch along, one percentage point at a time.

"This is taking too long," Nicole said impatiently as the meter hit 50 percent complete.

"The files you want are huge." Zoey looked up from the computer screen and saw Nicole pacing back and forth. "So, cool your jets and sit down. It will be done when it's done. You wearing a hole in the carpet isn't gonna make it go any faster."

Instead of sitting down, Nicole stood by the door and peeked out. "Hallway is clear," she said, thinking about making their escape once the files had finally been downloaded.

"And if they weren't clear, Garrika would have told us. So, I say again, cool your jets, sit down, and relax. We're at 70 percent," Zoey said, and Nicole sat.

Usually, she would have been as cool as the proverbial cucumber, but Nicole wasn't in control of the operation, a position she was unfamiliar with and uncomfortable with. However, with absolutely no choice in the matter, she had to relax and trust her team.

"Done," Zoey finally said and sent Garrika a text.

We're done. Status of exit?

You are clear to exit the office and make your way along the prearranged route to the maintenance entrance.

"Let's go," Zoey said, and they left the office, heading for the exit. Garrika stayed in her position until she received Zoey's text.

We're out.

At that point, Garrika went to the maintenance entrance and exited the building without issue. With her task completed, she went home while Nicole and Zoey went back to Zoey's house to what she called her operation center and went to work.

"The encryption on these files is the next level. It's going to take me some time to access them."

"I understand. Are you hungry? I know I am."

"I am too. I thought about meeting in the cafeteria for lunch, but it might attract attention to us. You know, three people nobody had seen before all having lunch together."

"I hear you. And that's all it would take for some busybody to call security. Good call. So, what do you have a taste for?"

"I'm a burger girl from birth."

"I can do a burger. Do you have a spot in mind? I'll go pick it up."

"Bronx Burger House on Mosholu Avenue. And I know what I want."

"What's that?"

"Old English burger. It has applewood smoked bacon and cheddar, and they serve it on an English muffin."

"Got you," Nicole said, grabbed her keys, and headed out.

She chose the cowboy burger with jalapeños, caramelized onions, pepper jack cheese, bacon, mushrooms, and chipotle aioli, then returned to Zoey's operation center with the food. When she arrived, Zoey was still hard at work decrypting the files. It was well into the following day before she could crack the encryption on the files.

"Finally," Zoey said and woke up Nicole. "I'm in." She got up from the computer. "It's all yours. I'm going to bed. Knock on my door if you need anything."

"Thanks, Zoey," Nicole said, sitting at the computer and digging into the files to get the information she sought.

Chapter 37

Nicole had been reviewing the information that Zoey gave her access to for hours, and she had barely scratched the surface. She had spent a great deal of time on the files belonging to Nigel Paris and Roston Brathwaite. It became evident to her that Emil Dudenhoeffer wasn't just the high-priced lawyer who kept them out of serving serious prison time for the crimes and other atrocities they'd committed. Emil Dudenhoeffer was also the one who was giving them tasks to carry out and instructions on how to get them done.

But who's giving you orders? Nicole was left to wonder.

All that she had to go on were vague references to someone called "Chacho" and the initials "SA."

Could that be him?

She couldn't be sure. And even if she thought Chacho or SA was the head man, there was no way for her to be positive, so she kept reading. That was when Nicole came across a document that said Nigel Paris and Roston Brathwaite's current assignment was to find Alamilla Delgado and return her to Colombia.

She remembered seeing the name Alamilla Delgado while searching through all the files and data she had available to her. She went back, and sure enough, there was a video marked *Excerpt from Alamilla Delgado Therapist Session.*

After reviewing the information available—"The 27-year-old third child of Isabella and Santiago Delgado was born in Cartagena, Colombia, but migrated to New York when she was 10. No employment record and has no visible means of support,"—Nicole pressed play.

"Tell me what it's like being married to him," the therapist asked.

"Sometimes living with Chacho is wonderful. He can be so nice, considerate, and loving, and other times, most of the time, living with him is the nightmare that I can't wake up from. On those days, he is physically, verbally, and mentally abusive."

"Tell me about that."

"He grabs, he shakes, he slaps and punches me. Never in my face. No, no, never in 'that pretty face.' That's what he says. 'Wouldn't wanna mess up that pretty face, now would we?'"

A single tear cascaded down her cheek.

"I live each day in constant terror because I never know which Chacho he'll be that day. The lover or the nightmare." Alamilla dropped her head in her hands, and the tears flowed freely. The therapist gave her time to compose herself. She looked up.

"I remember this one time when we were going to an outdoor concert. It was hot that day, almost a hundred degrees, and I had picked out a sundress to wear, and he said, 'No, I want you to wear the blue dress.' I said it was too hot outside for the tight blue dress and that I was wearing the sundress. When I walked past him, he grabbed me by the hair and slung me across the room like a rag doll and onto the floor. And then he rushed at me, got in my face, and screamed, 'You're wearing the blue dress!' Then he saw the sundress I'd laid out on the bed. He ripped it apart with his bare hands, and then he went to my closet and got the blue dress that he

wanted me to wear and threw it at me. After that, he pulled me up by my shoulders and shook me. He kept saying, 'You will wear what I tell you,' and then he let me go and walked away."

"Did you put on the blue dress?"

"Of course I did. And when I was dressed, he came back into the room, kissed me like nothing had happened, and said I looked nice." Alamilla dropped her head. "I'd kill him if I got the chance."

"I didn't hear what you said."

Alamilla lifted her head. "I said I'd kill him if I ever got the chance."

The excerpt from the therapist session ended there. It left Nicole with the same question. Who is Chacho, and was he the head of the drug organization she'd been tracking for months? She shut down the computer and armed herself. There was one way that she could find an answer to her question. She had gotten the last known address in Brooklyn for Nigel Paris and Roston Brathwaite from the FBI files Zoey had hacked and got confirmation from Dudenhoeffer's files. That would be her next stop, and Nicole planned to reach out to Agent McCullough to see what she could tell her.

When she arrived in Brooklyn, Nicole found that the house was burned to the ground. That raised another question that she didn't have an answer to. *Are they dead or alive?* she questioned and drove away.

Her next stop was the Jacob K. Javits Federal Office Building at 26 Federal Plaza in Manhattan to the offices of the FBI.

"Good afternoon," the agent at the desk said. "How can I help you today?"

"Good afternoon, sir. Former FBI Special Agent Nicole Maddox to see FBI Special Agent McCullough, please. And I don't mind waiting."

The guard looked at Nicole. Naturally, he'd heard the name when she was charged with espionage and conspiracy against the United States and of her capture of radical white supremacist Bob Gividen and for uncovering the White America First plot to overthrow the government. He nodded in acknowledgment of her service to her country.

"Have a seat, Former Agent Maddox, and I will let Agent McCullough know you're here to see her."

"Thank you."

After a while, the former agent was escorted to a conference room, and shortly after that, Agent McCullough joined her there.

"Mac!" Nicole said and got up to shake her hand.

"How are you, Nicole?"

"Doing fine, Mac. How've you been doing? I see you made it back to the organized crime division."

"Yeah. As much fun as we had saving the free world from white supremacists, counterterrorism wasn't my jam. I am much happier here."

"I hear you."

"What about you? I know you left the Bureau. What are you into these days?"

"I work for the Department of Defense, and that's all I can say."

"What can I do for you?"

"I've been tracking a drug dealer who is using the drug profits to fund terrorist organizations in the Middle East and North Africa, and I ran across the name Chacho and the initials SA. I was hoping you could tell me about them."

"Him," McCullough corrected. "One guy. His name is Sanchez Aguilar."

"SA." Nicole nodded. "What can you tell me about him?"

"That he's practically a ghost. Our intel says that El Chacho and his Barichara Cartel are moving to become major players in the US drug market. But the DEA begs to differ."

"Why?"

"Because they can't find him or any evidence that his organization even exists. The interdiction efforts that they've undertaken focused on finding, disrupting, dismantling, and interrupting financial activities but have netted no results. However, our sources tell us that the Barichara Cartel has become a thorn in the side of the other cartels because they are selling a high-quality product at prices that are hard to compete with. That's about all I can tell you, Nicole."

She stood up. "Thanks, Mac."

Other than having a name, Nicole was no closer to finding Sanchez Aguilar than she had been when she walked in the door at 26 Federal Plaza. She left the building and went back to Zoey's house, thinking that there were two things that she needed to do.

"Find Nigel Paris and Roston Brathwaite, and find Alamilla Delgado," she told Zoey and saw the look on her face. "What?"

"You're not gonna find Paris and Brathwaite."

"Why not?"

"They're dead."

"How do you know this?"

"I know people who know people who know the people that killed them," Zoey reluctantly said.

"Who?"

"Mike Black."

"Who is Mike Black?"

"I think you need to talk to the Colonel about that."

Chapter 38

"I was just getting ready to call you," Carla said to Black when he called her first thing that morning.

"How are you this morning, Carla?"

"Doing fine, Mike. What about you?"

"I'm good. But now I'm wondering what you got for me."

"I'll tell you when I see you."

"We're on our way."

"See you when you get here."

"Should I tell Jake to get the jet ready?"

"You should call Jake."

"Thanks, Carla."

Just over an hour later, Black and Shy walked into the office where Carla was waiting.

"Good morning, Shy."

"Hey, Carla, how's it going?"

"Going good this morning." Carla got up, and they followed her into the server room. She picked up her tablet and tossed an image up on the big screen. "That is Alamilla Delgado."

"She's very pretty, Michael." Shy giggled. "The way things are going, I wouldn't be surprised if Elias was having an affair with her too."

"Neither would I," Black said, smiling.

"I could track her to the Meliá Punta Cana Beach wellness hotel. It's an adult-only resort. I've picked her up there a couple of times, but I can't say for sure that she's staying at the hotel. She's pretty good at avoiding cameras."

"It's a start," Black said, taking out his phone.

"Erykah Morgan."

"Erykah, it's Mike."

"Good morning, Mike. How are you this morning?"

"I'm good. But I need you to book me and Cassandra a suite at the Meliá Punta Cana Beach hotel in the Dominican Republic."

Erykah wrote down the name of the hotel. "Checking in?"

"Today. I don't know for how long."

"I'll book it for three days, and you can go from there," Erykah said.

"Sounds good. See you when I get back."

After leaving the office, Black and Shy went home to prepare for their Dominican Republic flight.

Jake landed at Punta Cana Airport, and they were taken to their hotel. Once they were checked into their suite, Shy went out on the balcony to enjoy the view.

"It's beautiful here."

Black stood behind her and wrapped his arms around her. "Almost as beautiful as you."

"You still say the sweetest things to me."

"All true, Mrs. Black. All true." He nuzzled her neck. "Maybe we'll come back here and spend a few days."

"I'd like that."

"Now, Alamilla Delgado. How do you find somebody who doesn't wanna be found?"

"I have no idea. How do you usually find somebody who doesn't wanna be found?"

"We threaten to kill people until somebody tells me what I wanna know."

"Well, there you go." Shy separated herself from her husband's embrace. "Let's go do that." Black and Shy left their suite and went out into the hotel.

Since Carla couldn't verify that Alamilla Delgado was actually staying in the hotel, that would be the first thing they did. Armed with the image of Alamilla Delgado and money, of course, Shy showed the image to the people at the reception desk.

"Have you seen this woman here at the hotel?"

Both the man and the woman at the reception desk looked at the image. "I haven't seen her," the man said, returning to his duties.

The woman looked closely at the image. "I've seen her."

"Is she staying here at the hotel?"

"I don't think so. I mean, I don't remember her checking in. But it's possible that someone else could have checked her in." She handed Shy back the image.

"Thank you," Shy said and looked around for Black. She found him in one of the bars talking to the bartender.

"Did you find out anything?" she asked.

"He's seen her but doesn't think she's staying here because she pays for her drinks in cash and does not charge it to a room. What about you?"

"Same. The receptionist said she'd seen her but didn't check her in."

"Okay. Let's assume she's not staying here, but people have seen her here, so I think she's staying somewhere nearby and is just using the resort"—he chuckled—"like a resort."

With that thought in mind, Mr. and Mrs. Black spent the remainder of the evening in the hotel, at the bars, in the restaurants, and at the pool, and they hung around the lobby until well after midnight, hoping that Alamilla Delgado would make an appearance, but she didn't.

"Let's go get some sleep, and we'll get on it in the morning," Black said. They finally retired to their suite. "And maybe do something to find her other than hope she just shows up," he said as the elevator closed.

In the morning, Shy dressed in a red Moschino halter jumpsuit, and they were getting ready to go to have breakfast and expand their search when someone knocked at the door. Shy went to answer.

"Cassandra Black?"

"Yes. Can I help you?"

"My name is Nicole Maddox. I work for Colonel Mathis."

The mere mention of the Colonel brought back memories of Italy.

Shy had completed the task the Colonel had asked of her and taken the first steps to start her business. She was on her way back to the hotel when her driver slammed on the brakes because the car in front of them stopped abruptly, and they slammed into it.

When the driver of the other car got out, he raised a weapon and shot her driver. A van pulled up alongside them, and two Arab men jumped out. Napoleon hit the man who killed their driver and then turned to the other man who was about to open Shy's door. He fired and killed him, and then Napoleon dropped to the ground as the remaining shooter opened fire on him.

Shy and Napoleon stayed low to the ground as two more men got out of the vehicle in front of them and began firing at them with semiautomatic weapons. Once they made it to better cover behind a car parked on the street, they both opened fire at their attackers, but they were seriously outgunned.

When Shy ducked into the lobby of a building to reload her Beretta, she watched as her pursuers entered the building. Shy ran up the steps to the fourth floor before she stopped. She saw different men exiting the elevator when she stepped into the hallway. Once they turned and saw Shy with her gun in hand, one raised his silencer-clad weapon and took a shot at her.

Shy ran in the opposite direction, rounded the corner, and entered the first unlocked office she could find. Who are these guys? She locked the door, leaned against it, and breathed deeply.

"Sandy?"

"Aunt Evelyn?" *Shy looked up that day in Palermo and was shocked to see her aunt Evelyn.*

"What are you doing here?"

"Today, I'm an operative of the United States government."

"What did you say?" Shy asked again, even though she'd heard what Nicole said.

"I said my name is Nicole Maddox, and I work for Colonel Mathis. Can I come in?"

Shy stepped aside and allowed Nicole into their suite, wondering what one of the Colonel's operatives would be doing there.

"Thank you," Nicole said as Shy closed the door. She saw Black sitting there, looking just as curious as Shy.

"Michael, this is Nicole Maddox. She works for Colonel Mathis."

"Well, come in and have a seat."

"Thank you, Mr. Black."

"Please, call me Mike."

"Then it has to be Nicole."

"What can we do for you and the Colonel, Nicole?"

"It's more what we can do for each other."

"I'm listening," Black said, and Shy came and sat beside him.

"It seems we're tracking the same person in the Dominican Republic." Nicole paused. "Sanchez Aguilar."

Neither Black nor Shy said anything.

"We're both here looking for Alamilla Delgado so she can lead us to him."

"If you don't mind me asking, what's the Colonel's interest in him?"

"Sanchez Aguilar is a drug dealer who is using some of his proceeds to fund terrorists. My mission is to find him and stop him." Nicole looked between Black and Shy. "So, if you don't mind me asking, what's *your* interest in him?"

"He had my brother killed, and I want to know why." Black looked into Nicole's eyes. "My mission is to kill him. Does the Colonel have a problem with that?"

"Not at all. Like I said, we can help each other."

At that point, Shy had heard enough. Remembering that their last encounter with Colonel Mathis nearly got them both killed, she stood up.

"Thank the Colonel for us, but we'll be fine on our own," she said, and both Black and Nicole looked at her.

"Okay." Nicole stood up. "But I know where Alamilla Delgado is hiding. So, you could come with me, and we can both find out what we wanna know. Or not. Your choice."

Now Shy looked between Black and Nicole.

"I'll go get my guns."

Chapter 39

Once Shy had armed herself, she, Black, and Nicole left their suite at the Meliá Punta Cana Beach hotel. They took the elevator to the lobby and exited through the main entrance. Then Nicole surprised Black and Shy when she kept walking past the parking lot.

"Where are you parked?" Shy asked.

"Oh. Did I forget to mention it's not far from here?"

"You did," Shy said.

"It's easier to walk."

Nicole was as good as her word because they were walking into the Garden Suites a few minutes later and went to one of the bungalows. Black knocked on the door.

"Alamilla Delgado," he said when she opened the door. "My name is—"

"Mike Black." She stepped aside to allow them into the bungalow. She laughed a little and closed the door. "Elias said you would come. You look a lot like him."

"This is my wife, Cassandra."

"Shy. Nice to meet you."

"And this is Nicole Maddox."

"Nicole."

"Are you all right?" Black asked.

"I'm okay, I guess. Just wondering how you found me."

"That's not important right now," Nicole said.

"What's important is your safety," Shy stated.

Alamilla walked away from the door. "I'll never be safe as long as Chacho is alive," she said and sat down in the living room of her bungalow.

"We'll see about that," Black replied as he sat across from her. Shy sat next to him. "But I need to know why Sanchez Aguilar or Chacho or whoever the fuck he calls himself had my brother killed."

"It's a long story." Alamilla sighed and dropped her head. And then she looked up at Nicole and smiled. "Elias and I were in love."

Shy leaned close to Black. "Told you," she whispered.

"I told Chacho I needed a break from him, but I knew I was done with him. I could not take any more of his abuse. So I went to Miami. That's where I met and fell in love with Elias. We were so happy together. It was like my life had begun again, and the nightmare I'd been living was over. But I was wrong." She paused.

"After a while, we were planning to leave Miami and come to New York, when Chacho came for me and forced me to return with him. I thought I'd never see Elias again, but he found me." Alamilla smiled as she thought about the day they spent together. "I was back in hell, and seeing Elias, even if it was just for the day, was wonderful. I don't know what I was thinking. A show of defiance . . . I don't know, but I took Elias to the fields that day."

"The coca fields?" Nicole questioned.

"Yes."

"And you know where they are?" Nicole inquired.

"Would you like the coordinates?"

"Yes, I would very much like the coordinates to the fields."

"But we tripped an alarm," she said as she wrote down and handed Nicole the information. "I told Elias to run, and I would meet him in New York. But when I returned to the house, his foremen told Chacho that he'd seen us together. And he knew."

That was when Alamilla started to cry.

"He knew what, Alamilla?" Black asked.

"I wasn't feeling well, so I had gone to the doctor a couple of days before that," she said as tears rolled down her cheeks. "And that's how he found out."

"Found out what?"

"My doctor called and told Chacho that I was five weeks pregnant." Silence filled the room as Black, Shy, and Nicole absorbed what they had just heard. Shy leaned close to Black.

"Told you," she whispered.

"I had just returned from being gone almost two months, so he knew the baby wasn't his. He was furious. He tried to kill me." Her tears were flowing freely now. "His hands were around my throat. If it wasn't for Enrique pulling him off me, I would have died that day." Alamilla took a deep breath. "So I ran." She bravely wiped away her tears. "Several days later, I called Elias at his hotel, and a detective answered the phone and told me he was dead. I've been here ever since."

"We got to get you outta here," Shy said.

"Get packed," Black said.

"I never unpacked." Alamilla stood up and began moving toward the bedroom. "I've been living out of my suitcase since I left Colombia."

When Alamilla returned with her suitcase, Shy stood up and went to the door. She stepped outside and came right back in.

"What's wrong?" Black asked.

"Two SUVs just pulled up with eight men. And yes, they have guns," she said, taking the weapon from her purse.

Black looked at Alamilla. "Go in the bathroom and get in the tub," he said, and she ran off. "Cassandra, take the high ground. Open up when you're set."

Shy took the PLR22 and ran up the stairs to the loft.

Black turned over the couch. "You and me can pick them off when they come through the door," he said to

Nicole, and they took cover behind the sofa. They pointed their weapons at the door and waited.

Shy had a clear shot of the men from her position in the loft window as they approached the house. She fired the second they were in range and took out one target. They separated and ran toward the house. She was able to shoot another before they kicked in the door.

When the men came through the door, Black shot one, and Nicole shot another before the next man barged through the door and began firing at them with an AK-47. Black and Nicole dove for cover.

"Cassandra, get down here!" Black shouted as bullets bounced off the wall behind them.

Suddenly, Shy appeared at the top of the steps and fired. She hit another of the gunmen, and that allowed Black and Nicole to shoot and kill the last two men.

With the shooting over, Shy came down the stairs. "Everybody all right?"

"I'm good." Nicole got to her feet.

"I'm all right."

"I'm going to check on Alamilla," Shy said and walked toward the rear of the bungalow. That was when she saw a man dragging Alamilla out the back door. He fired at Shy.

"They're taking her out the back!" she yelled, ducking behind a wall for cover and then returning fire.

Shy came out from cover and went after them, firing shots as she ran. An SUV pulled up, and the man put Alamilla in the backseat. He fired several shots at Black and Nicole as they ran out the back door before he got in the SUV, and they drove off with Alamilla. Shy ran into the street and fired more shots that hit the back of the SUV as it sped away.

As they watched the SUV race out of sight, Black and Nicole sat on the curb. Shy came and joined them.

"What now?" Shy asked.

"I'm going to find those fields," Nicole said.

"What are you gonna do when you find them?" Black asked.

"I don't know yet. But I'm sure I'll think of something."

"What about us, Michael? What are we gonna do?"

"Ain't a damn thing change. He's still gotta die for killing Elias."

"Yeah, but how are we gonna find him? We lost Alamilla," Shy pointed out.

"I think I know somebody I could call to make that happen."

"Who?"

Chapter 40

After losing Alamilla, Black, Shy, and Nicole returned to their suite at the hotel.

"I could use a drink," Nicole said.

"Me too," Shy cosigned. "We're going down to the bar."

"Go ahead. I'll be down there soon," Black said, and once the ladies were gone, he took out his phone. His first call was to Rain.

"This Rain."

"What's going on up there?"

"Everything's been quiet since you left."

"That's good. You hear from Angelo?"

"I did. What do you want me to do?"

"Your choice. You can meet with them or stall them until I get back."

"When you coming back?"

"I don't know."

"I'll meet with them. I wouldn't want them to think we're avoiding them."

"Okay."

"How's it going with you?"

"We found her, and then we lost her."

Rain laughed. "So, what's the plan now?"

"Get her back. It's the *how* part that I haven't figured out yet."

"I know you'll think of something. You always do."

"Right. I'll see you when I get back," Black said, ending the call with Rain and making another call. It took a while, but he finally came to the phone.

"When they told me that Mike Black was on the line holding for me, I could hardly believe my ears. How are you, my friend?"

"I'm great, and yourself?"

"I have no complaints to speak of."

"I need to talk to you."

"Are you coming down?"

"I am."

"Are you bringing your wife?"

"I am."

"Excellent. This time you will be a guest in my home. When should I expect you?"

"Tomorrow."

"I will have a car meet you."

"Sounds good, my friend. See you tomorrow."

Jake had the jet ready the following morning, and Mr. and Mrs. Black were about to board.

"Are you sure we can't drop you off somewhere?" Black asked Nicole.

"No, I'll be fine."

"Okay, then." Black held out his hand. "It was good to meet you."

"Likewise. It was even better working with you," Nicole said and shook hands with Black and Shy.

"Give my best to the Colonel," Shy said, getting on the jet.

"Good luck."

"Same to you," Nicole said, and Black got on the jet.

Nicole stood and watched as Jake taxied down the runway and took off before she left.

Caracas, Venezuela

It was late afternoon when Jake landed the Cessna at Simón Bolívar International Airport of Maiquetí in

Caracas. The city is officially named Santiago de León de Caracas, Venezuela's capital and its largest city. It is located in the country's northern part and follows the Cordillera de la Costa contours on the Venezuelan coastal mountain range. Black and Shy had traveled to Caracas to see Rodrigo Iñíguez.

As Jake taxied and brought the aircraft to a stop, Shy looked out the window and saw the limousine waiting and a woman standing beside it.

"Good afternoon, Mr. and Mrs. Black. And welcome back to Caracas."

"Thank you," Black said.

"I am Romina del Valle Garcia, Mr. Iniquez's assistant."

"Yes, Ms. Garcia. I remember you from the last time Michael and I were here. How have you been?" Shy asked.

"I am fine. Thank you very much for asking. If you would follow me, I'll take you to Mr. Iñiquez."

Once their luggage was seen to, Romina had the driver take them to the house. They drove along the Venezuelan coastal mountain range.

"We're not going to his house?" Black asked Romina as they drove past Iñíguez's mansion.

"Yes, Mr. Black. We are going to Mr. Iñíguez's house. He recently moved."

"I see," Black said as they slowed down in front of and stopped at a smaller beachfront home a few houses away from the mansion. His old residence was a fifteen-bedroom, ten-bath mansion, but this house was half the size, with only five bedrooms and three bathrooms. While somebody saw to their luggage, Romina escorted Black and Shy out to a large balcony with a bar. The cliffside view of the Caribbean from there was breathtaking.

At a small table nearby sat Rodrigo Iñíguez. He sprang to his feet when he saw them. "Mike, Cassandra. How are you doing today? And welcome to my home."

"Thank you for having us, Rodrigo," Shy said as Romina disappeared.

He hugged Shy and shook hands with Black. "And you, Mike, how are you?"

"I am fine," Black said.

"Please, have a seat."

"Thank you, Rodrigo," Shy said.

"Can I get you something to drink?"

"Thank you, Rodrigo," Black said, and Rodrigo went to the bar.

"That was Don Q Gran Anejo on the rocks for the lady and Rémy Martin Louis XIII in a glass for the gentleman," Rodrigo said, smiling as he poured and then served them their drinks before joining them at the table. It was then that Romina returned to the balcony with a woman and a young child. Once again, Rodrigo got to his feet and waved her over.

"It is my honor to introduce you to my wife, Jahaziel, and my son, Reinier."

"Your son?" Black asked in surprise. "Congratulations," he said, knowing how badly Rodrigo wanted a son.

"Thank you, thank you," Rodrigo said and nodded to Jahaziel.

"*Encantado de conocerte,*" Jahaziel said and returned to the house.

"Sorry, she doesn't speak any English," Rodrigo said. He looked at Black and Shy and shrugged his shoulders. "She gave me a son. I gave her my name."

"You'll forgive me for asking, but what happened to Ximena?" Shy asked.

"She divorced me. Over Reinier."

"I'm sorry."

"Believe me, Cassandra, so am I." Rodrigo dropped his head a bit. "She was willing to tolerate my many indiscretions, but the boy—" He shook his head. "That, she could not stand for. You see, one bright, sunny afternoon, Jahaziel came to my home, and when Ximena answered the door, she said, 'This is your husband's son.' I had no knowledge of the boy, and I didn't know who Jahaziel was. I remember being at the event more than I remember being with her. But she gave me a son, an heir, so, as I said, when Ximena divorced me, I gave Jahaziel my name. But not my heart, Cassandra. I don't love her. There is only one woman that I love. Unfortunately, it took this to make me realize it."

"What happened to Ximena?" Shy asked.

"She still lives in the house with my daughters." He paused. "Which brings me to a question. Two, actually. How long are you planning to be here?"

"I'm not sure," Black said.

"I see." Rodrigo glanced at Shy. "If you will be here for a while, I am sure Ximena would love to see you. Now, my second question is, why are you here?"

"Do you know Sanchez Aguilar?"

Rodrigo frowned. "Yes, I know Chacho. Why?"

"Do you think you could introduce us?"

"Yes. I can do that. But why do you want to meet Chacho?"

"He had my brother murdered."

Rodrigo nodded. "That was your brother?"

"Yes."

"Then you intend to kill him."

"Yes."

"Easier said than done, my friend. He is quite well protected, especially at his home."

"You let me worry about that. Will you do it?"

"Of course." Rodrigo laughed. "He's an arrogant fuck who deserves to die. He has made very many enemies in a short space of time."

"So I've heard."

"His people are pushing their way into Miami, Atlanta, and New York with a quality product that he sells cheaply. You'll be doing the world a favor. I will make the call, but first,"—Rodrigo stuck one finger in the air—"we dine."

Rodrigo escorted them to the dining room, where his cook had prepared a feast fit for kings and queens. After dining on a buffet that included many Venezuelan dishes, pabellón criollo, cachitos, arepas, Venezuelan tequeños, and caraotas negras, Romina entertained Mr. and Mrs. Black on the balcony. At the same time, Rodrigo excused himself to make the call. When he returned to the balcony, he had a smile on his face.

"It's all arranged. You and your lovely wife will meet him at his home in Valledupar tomorrow."

"Thank you, Rodrigo," Black said.

Chapter 41

Somewhere in the Colombian Andes Mountains

Nicole watched from the window of the abandoned gas station as the Grey Wolf helicopter landed outside. When she saw a man disembark, she went out to greet him.

"Nicole?"

"Yes."

"I'm Captain Liam Giannantonio, US Air Force retired."

"Good to meet you, Captain. What's our status?"

"She's racked and ready with four intercontinental conventional ballistic missiles."

"Here are the coordinates," Nicole said, handing him the paper with the location of Sanchez Aguilar's coca field.

He nodded. "Watch your head," he said. They walked to the aircraft, and once the captain went over his checklist and reviewed his safety concerns with Nicole, they got underway.

"According to these coordinates, we're here."

"Take us down. I wanna get a closer look," Nicole said, and he took the aircraft to a level just above the trees. A green net covered the fields, which would appear to be trees from satellite or aerial surveillance. "Take us to a safe firing range and fire when ready."

"Missile one locked on target."

"Fire!"

The missile hit its intended target, and it exploded into flames.

"Missile two locked on target."

"Fire!"

When the missile hit its target, it burst into flames, and the fire spread.

"Take us around. I wanna get a closer look at the damage. Make sure we got it all," Nicole said, and he took the aircraft for a pass around the field. "Let's drop the rest of our load and call it a day."

"On our way for a second run."

"Fire when ready."

"Missile three locked on target."

"Fire!" Nicole said and watched the missile hit its intended target, explode into flames, and the fire spread.

"Missile four locked on target."

"Fire," Nicole said, and with one more pass, they headed back.

Valledupar, Colombia

Alamilla Delgado opened her eyes and quickly had to shield them from the morning sun. She lay there for a while, thinking about what would happen to her next. She hadn't seen Chacho since they dragged her back to this prison and hoped she could go another day before she did. She got out of bed, walked out on the balcony overlooking the garden, and inhaled deeply as she looked over the vast property.

It's a pretty prison, at least, she thought and then went back inside. There was a light tap on the door.

"Come in."

"Good morning, Alamilla," Luisa, her personal maid, said.

"Morning, Luisa."

"Would you like me to run your bath?"

"Not just yet, Luisa. I want to get some coffee first," Alamilla said, walking toward the door.

"Yes, ma'am."

"You're my age, Luisa. You don't have to call me ma'am," she said and left the room, surprised that there were no guards outside her door.

"Yes, ma'am."

Her first thought was to run away again. But that would be futile because Chacho would find her and send men to drag her back once more. Alamilla wandered through the mansion that was rumored to have once been one of the secret residences of former President Mariano Ospina Pérez. However, there was no proof of that. She walked into the kitchen.

"Good morning, Alamilla," Maria, the cook, said. She, along with Enrique, the butler, ran the house.

"Good morning, Maria," she said, going to the coffee pot.

"Would you like something to eat?"

"No, just coffee."

"You haven't eaten since you've been back. Let me make you some arepas with butter and quesito."

"No, thank you, Maria. Just coffee," she said as she poured a cup.

"I made some mote de guineo earlier. I could make some for you," Maria said as Enrique entered the kitchen. Alamilla smiled when she saw him. He was her savior, having pulled Chacho off her so many times in the past. She wondered how long it would be before he had to save her again.

"Good morning, Alamilla."

"Good morning, Enrique."

"It's good to have you home," he said. Enrique had come to love her like she was one of his own daughters.

"I wish I could say it's good to be home."

"Mr. Chacho would like to see you in his study."

"I'll be there after I bathe," Alamilla said, walking out of the kitchen.

"I'm sorry, Alamilla, but he wants to see you now. He was most insistent."

"Okay, Enrique," she said, walking with him to the study. He opened the door for her to enter.

"Thank you, Enrique. When Mr. and Mrs. Black arrive, bring them here," Chacho said.

"Yes, sir," Enrique said, bowing slightly before he shut the door.

"Your would-be rescuers are coming," he said as the phone rang. "*Hola.*"

"The fields are on fire!" his foreman, Mateo, shouted.

"What?"

"I said the fields are on fire!"

"Slow down, Mateo, and tell me what happened," Chacho said, his heart racing.

"There was a loud noise, and then the fields were on fire. It spread to the plant."

"Was anybody hurt?"

"No, but the fire did a lot of damage."

Chacho was shocked, thinking about being ruined, and dropped the phone.

"Hello, hello!" Mateo shouted, but Chacho had slumped down in the chair at the head of the table.

Meanwhile, Black and Shy arrived at the Aguilar home. Enrique greeted them.

"Mike and Cassandra Black to see Mr. Aguilar."

"Yes. Mr. Aquilar is expecting you. If you would please follow me, I'll take you to him," Enrique said, leading the way.

As they walked a few feet behind Enrique, Shy leaned close to Black. "What are you gonna do?"

"I don't know."

"You don't know?"

"I'm working it out as we go."

"I don't like the sound of that. Have you figured out how we're getting outta here?"

"Working that out too," Black said as they arrived at the study.

Enrique tapped once on the door before he opened it and stepped into the room. They were all shocked to see Alamilla standing behind the chair where Chacho was sitting. She had a knife in her hand and was stabbing Chacho repeatedly in the chest.

"Alamilla, no!" Enrique shouted as Alamilla put the knife to his neck, held on to his forehead, then slit Chacho's throat.

Enrique rushed to her, shouting, "Maria! Maria!"

Enrique took the knife from Alamilla as Maria rushed into the study.

"Why are you yelling like that, Enrique?" she questioned, and then she saw Chacho's bloody body slumped in the chair and blood on Alamilla's hands. "*Dios mío.*" She crossed herself. "*Dios mío.*"

"Take Alamilla out of here," Enrique said.

As Maria led Alamilla out of the study, Enrique turned to Black and Shy. "I think it's best that you leave."

"I think you're right," Black said.

"We'll show ourselves out," Shy said, quickly following her husband out of the study. They walked through the house as fast as possible. When they got outside, the limousine that had brought them there was still parked nearby, and the driver was standing by.

"Take us back to the airport," Black said as he opened the door for Shy to enter.

"And we're kind of in a hurry," Shy said.

Once the driver was in the limousine and drove way, Black took out his phone.

"What's up, Mike?"

"We're on our way, and we're coming in hot," Black said, letting Jake know he needed the jet ready to take off as soon as they were aboard.

Chapter 42

After recovering from her wounds, the day had come for Barbara to return to work. That morning, Destiny came and picked her up for the drive. It didn't take Barbara long to realize that Destiny wasn't headed toward the office.

"Where are you going, Dest?"

"To our new office." Destiny paused. "We thought . . . well, Michelle thought that with everything that happened, maybe you wouldn't want to . . . you know . . . be in that space. We agreed, so we rented some new office space."

"That was very considerate of you guys. I wasn't looking forward to it," Barbara said, and an image of Tahanee's body flashed in her mind. She quickly forced it away.

"This is it."

"Wow," Barbara exclaimed as Destiny pulled into the parking lot of a two-story building.

When they entered the building, Barbara saw the huge WELCOME BACK, BARBARA sign in the lobby that was positioned over a table with a small buffet spread: coffee, bagels, a meat platter, cream cheeses, jellies, and donuts. Suddenly, Michelle, Jolina, and Kayla appeared from behind the table.

"Welcome back!" they shouted.

"Thank you," Barbara said. "It's good to be out of the house."

After hugs and words of well wishes were expressed, they each helped themselves to the buffet.

"Come on, Barbie. Let me show you to your new office," Jolina said, grabbing Barbara by the hand and leading her to the elevator.

When they reached the second level, Jolina led Barbara to a large office on the front side of the building with a view of the street. "This is you, Barbie," she said excitedly.

"This is nice. I love it. Thank you for being so considerate. Like I was telling Destiny, I was feeling some kinda way about going to the old office and thinking about making a move." She looked at Michelle. "Thank you."

After a while, Destiny, Jolina, and Kayla drifted off to their new offices and left Michelle alone with Barbara.

"Dest told me that this was your idea."

"It was. I just thought about what happened and whether I would want to return to the place day after day, and the answer was no. So, I started looking."

"I love it." Barbara paused. "Is the entire building ours?"

"Yes. It was for sale. It's approximately 40,000 square feet, has two stories, and has retail and office space that spans approximately 30,000 square feet, with plenty of dedicated parking. I thought we could rent some of the space, and since it has that prominent retail space on the front, we could open another High-End Fashions store. I took a one-year option." Michelle paused. "What do you think?"

"I love it. I think it's an excellent move for us. Thank you, Michelle, for this and everything else you did while I was gone."

"I hope I didn't overstep."

"You did. You definitely overstepped when you gave the order for Axe to kill Adams without running it by me or Jackie or Rain."

Assuming she was about to be reprimanded for her actions, Michelle got quiet, her enthusiasm waned, and she prepared to get taken down a couple of notches.

"But fuck it. I asked you to step up, and you stepped up in a big way. I appreciate it, and I'm proud of you."

"Thank you, Barbara."

"Now, let's talk about where you see us fitting into your urban revitalization plan for the building you bought."

Michelle looked a little confused. "I work for you until somebody tells me differently, Barbara. My father said that when you're a hustler, you always gotta look for ways to make money and capitalize on opportunities for your crew and the Family. This is all yours, and we'll have our hands in all of it."

Barbara nodded. "What about the illegal activity? What's your plan for that?"

"Who's your best man?"

"Axe. No doubt."

"Put him in charge of organizing and creating new opportunities."

"What about the drugs?"

"We organize that too. The Family has people. I'm talking about Leon Copeland and Nina Thomas. I'm sure they will gladly pick up that business."

"Have you talked to Jackie about any of this?"

"No. Like I said, Barbara, I work for you."

"Your father taught you well," Barbara said, satisfied with the work her loyal soldier put in for her in her absence.

After work, Michelle had planned for the celebration to continue. She'd made reservations for them at La Grande Boucherie, a pricey French restaurant with a dining gallery that featured forty-foot glass ceilings. After dinner, they planned to go to Purple Rock to see Cristal.

"That's some bullshit," Barbara said. "I tried to get Cristal to play The House but was told Cristal didn't play small venues."

"Yeah, well, you're not Rain Robinson," Kayla said as the ladies dined on entrecôte grillée, faux-filet bercy, saucisse purée, filet de boeuf, and filet mignon au poivre.

At Purple Rock, RJ, Venus, Marvin, Judah, Baby Chris, and Payton Cummings arrived and were met by Rose. She had been the manager at JR's for years. Rain trusted her. Therefore, when she bought Purple Rock, Rain brought Rose over to manage the place, leaving Demi to run JR's.

"Is everything ready?" RJ asked Rose.

"I have a front-row center table all set up for your party," she said, leading the way to the table.

Meanwhile, backstage at Purple Rock, Anthony Quinn, a.k.a. Tone, a.k.a. Undisputed Truth, sat alone in his dressing room. Things had been breaking his way lately, and he was happy about that.

Terrell Sanders was dead. And now that Tone wasn't at his beck and call, he had a chance to live. It allowed him to focus on his music and relationship with Aurora Piper for the first time.

He had only seen Curtis a few times since Terrell Sanders ordered them to kill Barbara. He discussed putting something together the last time he saw him, but Tone hadn't heard from him since—something else he was happy about. But that was about to change.

Someone knocked on the door.

"Come in."

The stage manager stuck his head in the door. "You got a guest," he said, and Curtis walked in.

"What's up, Tone?"

"'Sup?" Tone said, not happy at all to see Curtis.
"Come on. We got work to put in."
"No."
"No? Fuck you mean, no?"
"I mean no. I'm about to go on. And," Tone paused. "I'm done with that life."
"What?"
"You heard me. I'm done."
"What you think this shit, these little three songs Hayven lets you do, make you a rap star? You think it's gonna get you paid? Well, think again, nigga. This is what's gonna get you paid." Curtis looked at Tone. "Go ahead and do your little set, but the second it's over, we're outta here to put in this work," Curtis said and walked out of the dressing room.

Meanwhile, out in the club, Barbara and her party arrived at Purple Rock and were seated by Rose. Barbara was sitting at the center of the table next to her brother, and she insisted that Michelle sit beside her. RJ stood and proposed a welcome-back toast to Barbara, and it was then that she saw Curtis coming out from backstage. She leaned closer to RJ.

"I think that's the man who shot me."
"Where?"
"Standing over by the stage entrance."

RJ and Barbara stood up and started heading toward the stage. He tapped Marvin on the shoulder as they walked.

"Walk with us, Money," he said, and Marvin followed RJ and Barbara away from the table.

As they got closer, Curtis looked and was shocked to see the woman he thought he'd killed walking toward him.

"That's Curtis," RJ said to Marvin. They'd been hunting him since they talked to Dashanique. When Curtis started running toward the exit, RJ and Marvin followed him.

He ran out of Purple Rock and down the street. Curtis pulled out his gun, turned, and fired off a couple of wild shots that hit nothing before he turned and started running again. When he ran into an alley and tried to climb the fence, Marvin grabbed him and slammed Curtis to the ground before he made it over.

RJ kicked him in the face and then stomped Curtis repeatedly. Then he grabbed Curtis and pulled him to his feet. He reached back and hit him. Curtis went down from the impact. Marvin picked Curtis up and threw him to the ground, hard.

Curtis got to his feet, and RJ hit him with blow after blow until he went down again. Then RJ stood over Curtis and kicked him a few times. Marvin pulled Curtis up again and rammed him face-first into the wall. He slammed Curtis's body into that wall over and over again until Curtis went down. RJ stood over him and began to stomp Curtis again. Then RJ got on top and hit Curtis several times in the face. He grabbed Curtis and began pounding his head into the ground, and a pool of blood quickly formed around his head. RJ hit him with lefts and rights to his face, wrapped his hands around Curtis's throat, and choked him until he slowly stopped moving and his body went limp.

Marvin pulled him off. "I think he's dead, RJ."

RJ kicked him one more time before he and Marvin walked back to Purple Rock.

Chapter 43

As Hayven Kawai belted out the song that would be the first single released from her album, Barbara watched RJ and Marvin chase Curtis out of Purple Rock before returning to her seat. She thought this was a situation of her own making, of her own arrogance. She may have been shot, but she was far from being the victim.

She had made herself a target.

It was Barbara who personally killed Raw-dog, the head of the G-40s. She disrespected and humiliated Montel Rigby, the head of the BBKs, to the point where when Ryder killed Truck. Instead of going after Ryder for what she'd done, Rigby took the BBKs to war against Barbara. Had it not been for Black assigning her captain, Jackie Washington, to run the war, Barbara would have had to fight them off.

With plenty of help, of course, but that wasn't the point.

When it became apparent to her that Terrell Sanders was just as responsible for Mason Grant's death as Willard Bellamy, she sent her men to kill him. And when they didn't get him, she should have had more protection.

As she reached the table, Barbara looked at Michelle. She had proven herself more than capable of running her legitimate business, and there was no question about her loyalty. Barbara's focus on building her legitimate business was a good thing. Good for Barbara. Good for the Family. It was good for all parties involved. But Barbara had to admit that she was a gangster. Everything she'd done in the Family spoke to that singular point.

And that made her a target. It made her realize that she always had to be on guard, or else the people she loved could die.

She'd been caught slippin', and it cost Tahanee her life. It would never happen again. Barbara decided then that Michelle could continue running her legitimate business, and she would solidify her position in the Family.

Barbara saw Rain coming. She'd observed the commotion. From this point forward, Barbara thought she needed to be more like Rain. Or better yet, she needed to be more like her idol—Shy.

Part businesswoman, part gangster, Barbara thought as Rain sat down next to her.

"What happened?" Rain asked as Baby Chris and Judah gathered around her.

"That was the man who shot me," Barbara said.

"You sure?" Judah asked.

"Yes, I'm sure."

When Hayven finished her song, the lights went out.

"Ladies and gentlemen . . . Undisputed Truth."

The spotlight appeared on Tone, and he broke into his first song to thunderous applause. Barbara leaned close to Rain and pointed at the stage.

"That's him!"

"What?" Rain asked.

"That's him!" Barbara pointed at the stage. "That's the other one."

Rain grabbed Barbara's hand. "Okay." She called Baby Chris and Judah over to her.

"What's up?" Baby Chris asked.

"That's the other muthafucka who shot Barbara. You two go to either side of the stage. As soon as his song is over, grab his ass and bring him to my office."

"On it," Judah said and walked off with Baby Chris.

"Come on, Barbara," Rain said.

As she followed Rain to her office, Barbara kept her eyes on Tone, but in her mind's eye, all she could see was Tahanee's body in the office. Suddenly, she began walking toward the stage. Tone saw her coming, and believing she was a fan, he went to the edge of the stage. But he froze when Barbara got close enough for him to recognize her.

"Oh, shit," he said as if it were part of the song.

He couldn't believe what he was seeing. They'd killed her. At least, that's what they thought. As he finished his song, he wondered how he would get out of this one. He looked to his left and saw Baby Chris inching closer. He started moving toward the other side of the stage to escape, but then he saw Judah on stage, closing in.

"Fuck it."

Tone dropped the microphone and jumped off the stage. He had brought his gun on stage to use as a prop during his performance. When Baby Chris and Judah jumped off the stage and went after him, Tone pulled out his gun. He turned and fired several shots at them. They hit the floor. Then Tone turned and began running toward the closest exit. A security guard stood at the exit. As Tone got closer to the guard, he raised the weapon, shot the guard, and ran out the door.

When Baby Chris and Judah came out of Purple Rock, Tone turned and fired. They took cover behind the dumpster as Tone reached his car, got in, and sped away. Baby Chris and Judah fired a few shots at the vehicle as it drove away, but they were out of range.

"I'll get the car!" Baby Chris shouted.

Judah watched the car to see which direction it went when Baby Chris pulled up alongside him in a brand-new Lotus Emira—a birthday gift from Payton. Judah got in, and Baby Chris stepped on it.

"This you?"

"Yeah. I don't drive it often, but tonight was a special occasion."

"Sweet."

"Do you see him?" Baby Chris asked.

Judah looked around the streets as Baby Chris drove. "We lost him."

Back inside Purple Rock, the stage show had stopped, and the DJ was playing music. Rain made her way backstage and went straight to Hayven Kawai's dressing room.

"I need the room," she said to Hayven's band members as she walked toward Hayven. When the last man closed the door behind himself, Rain took out her gun and held it to Hayven's head.

"Where's Tone?"

"I don't know."

"Where would he go?"

"He lives with a woman named Aurora, Aurora Piper," a scared-to-death Hayven shouted. She'd heard that the people who ran Purple Rock were gangsters, but she had never experienced it until now.

"Where do I find her?"

Hayven wrote down the address as quickly as she could and handed it to Rain, who snatched it from her hand.

"You know your boy killed somebody and shot another?" Rain said on her way to the door.

"I didn't know," Hayven said as Rain left her dressing room. She was glad to be alive and was now rethinking performing at Purple Rock.

Rain went to her office, where Barbara, Michelle, Jolina, Destiny, and Kayla were waiting. Everyone bounced to their feet when Rain entered.

"Come on, Barbara," she said, and Barbara left the office with Rain.

When Tone drove away from Purple Rock, he moved around, going nowhere fast, looking in his rearview mirror to see if Baby Chris and Judah were following him. Finally, he slowed down when he was sure that they weren't.

"What now?" Tone asked aloud.

The answer was, of course, simple. He needed to get away from there, out of the city, and as far away from New York as possible. Tone stopped at a red light and checked his weapon. He had no money, but he did have the means to get some. He planned to rob gas stations until he reached the South. "Go to Mississippi or Alabama."

He was all set to rob his first gas station when he thought about Aurora. If he was going on the run, he needed her with him. Tone started the car and drove to her apartment. On the way there, he took out his phone.

"Hey, baby. What's up?"

"We gotta get outta the city."

"Why? What's wrong?"

"I'll explain everything when I get there. But I need you to pack a bag, just the shit we need, and be ready when I get there."

"Okay," Aurora said, getting busy packing.

When he arrived at Aurora's apartment, she had packed a bag for each of them and was in the bathroom, frantically tossing toiletries into a bag. "Aurora!" he shouted when he came through the door. "You ready?"

"Almost," she shouted from the bathroom. "The bags by the door are ready."

Tone looked and saw the bags. "I'm gonna take these to the car."

"Okay. I'm almost ready," she said as Tone picked up the bags and left her apartment. He took the bags to the car, put them in the trunk, and had just closed it when he felt the barrel of a gun in his back.

"Move and die," Rain said, reaching around and taking Tone's gun from his waist. "Now, walk. Nice and slow."

At the point of Rain's gun, Tone walked to her car. Barbara was in the front passenger seat.

"Get in the back seat, Barbara," Rain ordered. "You drive," she said to Tone when Barbara got out.

Tone got in the car, and once Rain and Barbara were in, he drove off. They drove for a while until they passed a dark parking lot.

"Pull in there," Rain ordered, and Tone complied. "Stop here and get out."

Tone stopped the car, put it in park, and reached for the handle to get out. He thought about running and taking his chances. Rain put the barrel to the back of his head.

"Don't even think about it."

Rain got out and pointed the gun at Tone as Barbara got out.

"Walk," Rain ordered and gave Tone a little shove. He began walking but didn't get far.

"That's far enough," Barbara said, walking toward him, taking Rain's gun as she passed. "Turn around."

Tone turned, and Barbara looked him in the eyes. She thought about something her father said to her once. She had been in plenty of shootouts in her short time in the Family, but Bobby said it was different.

Standing before a man, looking him in the eyes, and then taking his life is something else entirely.

"This is for Tahanee." Barbara raised her weapon and shot Tone in the head. Then she stood over him and shot him three more times in the chest. "Rest in power, Tahanee."

Chapter 44

It had been a good day for Susan Beason. It was a long day but a good day all the same. She got up early, and once she was dressed in a Valentino Garavani crepe dress that showed off her amazing legs and a pair of Tom Ford Titan stiletto sandals that made her calves pop, she headed downtown to the law offices of Wanda Moore and associates to meet with her lawyers.

She had a criminal lawyer to keep her from going to jail. There was one lawyer to protect her from going broke and a divorce lawyer to get her out of this mess when it was all over. And for a change, each one had something good to tell her.

At her first meeting of the day, Susan and her criminal lawyer met with FBI investigator Connie Lewis. She had been investigating the failure of Emerson Savings and Loan and the sale to Daniel Beason. She had decided not to charge Susan with anything related to Daniel's defrauded investors, and she wouldn't have to assist in paying the settlement.

That meeting led perfectly to her next meeting with her financial lawyer. He had hired a forensic accountant to comb through Daniel's books and found where he had been hiding his money from her. Now that she didn't have to settle with his investors, that money was fair game for the divorce proceedings.

Her final meeting was a conference call with Daniel and his lawyer to hammer out the remaining sticking points in the contentious divorce. Armed with new information about his finances, Susan's lawyer went into the meeting in a position of strength, and to keep from going broke, Daniel agreed to Susan's terms.

"Daniel is signing the papers as we speak, and I will have a courier deliver them to your office," Susan heard his lawyer say, and the words were like music to her ears. She was free, or at least she would be, and she would come out of the mess as a very wealthy woman.

That night, Susan, dressed in a Cynthia Rowley neoprene jumpsuit, had been sitting out by the pool, sipping dirty dry gin martinis and gossiping on the phone with her girlfriend. After spending hours dragging other women through the mud, Susan decided to call it a night.

Susan got up and went into the house, thinking about the divorce proceeding against her husband, Daniel, and when it was all said and done, she would come out of it with the house *and* a big chunk of money.

When she was inside the house, she went into the kitchen to rinse her glass, but then she decided to have one more before turning in for the evening. Susan left the kitchen, entered the living room, and walked to the bar to make another pitcher of dirty dry gin martinis.

"You're starting to drink too much," she said aloud.

"Then maybe you should stop," a voice came from the room's darkness.

"Who said that? Who's in here?"

When a light came on in the living room, Angel Riddick was there. She was sitting on the couch with her Berretta on her lap.

"Who are you, and what are you doing in my house?"

"I'm here to kill you."

"What?"

Angel raised her weapon.

"Cassandra Black sends her regards," Angel said and shot Susan in the head.

When Susan's body dropped to the floor, Angel walked up, stood over her, and put two more shots in her chest. Then she left the house.